Collide and Burn

Franz Okuneva

Contents

Chapter 1

"Allison, hurry your ass up!" My mother calls from downstairs just as I'm throwing my hair up into a messy ponytail. I take in my appearance as I peer into the mirror, making sure I look okay. After being reassured that I look presentable, I roll my eyes at my mother's constant hollering.

I do have to get ready, I wish she would calm her nerves.

"I'm coming!" I call back, grabbing my backpack from beside my bed.

I find her in the kitchen, eating an apple at the wooden table and reading the newspaper. My mother has black and blond highlighted hair that stops in the middle of her back - since she always gets it trimmed - bright ocean blue eyes that are just a shade lighter than mine.

"Where's my breakfast?" I ask, as if my mother always makes breakfast for me. Yeah right. She doesn't even fix me an instant pancake on a stick.

"Where did you make it?" she throws back at me, not even glancing up from her stupid newspaper. My mother isn't a bad mother; she just doesn't baby me or fix me breakfast, obviously.

Looks like I'll be fending for myself, again.

"Ugh," I say, even though I'm not really mad and just to piss her off I grab her apple, taking a huge bite. "Love you," I walk out of the door with her apple in my hand, not bothering to give it back. That'll teach her to make me some damn breakfast.

I unlock the doors to my Camaro convertible, hopping in before crank-ing it up so I can look at my clock. Seven forty-five. Shit. It's the first day of junior year and I'm already half an hour late. I hope I don't have a Grinch as my homeroom teacher, 'cause I'm in deep shit if I do. I turn up my radio and P!nk instantly starts blasting.

I love her.

"So what!"

Stop at red light.

"I'm still a rock star."

Green light, go.

"I got my rock moves."

Press harder on the gas pedal.

"And I don't need you, tonight."

BANG!

Ah, shit! My car, my baby, you've got to be kidding me. I turn P!nk off as the shock of my baby Antoinette being hit settles in. Oh, no, no, no. I fling my car door open, ignoring the sunlight beaming down on me. I walk around to the front of my car and notice that it looks like half of the front of my car has been taken off. You've got to be shitting me! There are pieces of shattered glass on the ground from my broken headlights.

"Uh, that looks kind of bad," a deep husky voice says, and I turn around, instantly forgetting about my car. The hottest guy I've ever seen is standing in front of me, with shaggy dark brown hair, clover green eyes, sun-kissed skin and faint stubble. He's just over six feet tall with an obviously well-toned body.

Well-toned body?

What the hell!

He just hit Antoinette and I'm now checking him out...

Yes Allison, you've lost your damn mind, I think to myself.

Is that a tattoo I see?

Snap out of it!

"Kind of bad?... WHAT DO YOU MEAN 'KINDA' BAD?" I shriek when his words finally sink in, snapping back to reality. "You just hit my baby!"

He cringes away from me. "It wasn't my fault," he says, holding his hands up in surrender, which makes me concentrate on his face more. Well, I'll be damned, this isn't just some random hot guy, it's Blake Drayton - the school's supposed notorious bad boy and player.

I've seen him around school a couple of times and people are always talking about him. I think I actually had him in a couple of my classes last year and freshman year.

"What do you mean it wasn't your fault?" I cross my arms, not giving a damn who he is. He hit my car, and now I'm pissed.

"Exactly that. You're the one who ran into the stop sign," he points over my head, and I see the stop sign that I obviously didn't stop at.

Damn you P!nk and your amazing music!

"Well, why didn't you stop if you saw me coming?" I point an accusing finger at his chest. It's a nice chest by the way.

"Because I thought you were going to stop," he lets out a frustrated sigh, running a hand through his brown hair, messing it up but somehow making him look hotter. "Look, I'll pay for the damage," he tells me with a wave of his hand, already turning around to leave.

"Wait!" I call out, running after him and immediately regretting the action.

He abruptly turns around causing me to almost collide with his chest. "Yes?" He looks down at me as if I'm a bug he wants to squish.

"I need a ride to school now," I tell him, crossing my arms so it won't be too obvious that he's intimidating me.

He frowns, looking me over before looking at my car. "Okay, whatever," he turns around again and continues to walk to his car, a shiny black Ferrari that doesn't have a scratch on it, despite the fact that it just hit my car. How in the hell does it not have a scratch? I take a glance at Antoinette before running over to lock the doors and to make sure it's not directly in the street. I grab my bag and walk slowly over to Blake's car. I bet he doesn't even know who I am.

I open the passenger side door and see Blake waiting patiently as he starts to turn the knob on his radio. He glances over at me after I close my door before pulling off. Now that we're in the car together I feel nervous and wary.

Damn, what happened to courageous Allison?

"Legacy High, right?" Blake takes another glance at me before looking back at the road. So he's a safe driver. Shocker, since he ran into my car.

Well, okay it was my fault but who cares?

"Huh?" I ask, oblivious to what he said as I had been too absorbed in my own thoughts.

"You go to Legacy High, right?" There's a sound of annoyance in his tone which catches me off guard.

"Y-y-yeah," I stutter out, fidgeting with a bracelet on my wrist. So I'm intimidated by him again. This sucks ass!

"I'm Blake by the way," he says once we pull into the school parking lot. We're the only people out here, since everyone is already in homeroom. He pulls into a space close to the gym, but not too far from the school building.

"I'm Allison," I mutter, pulling my school schedule - that I received in the mail - out of my pocket. I open my car door and shut it with more force than necessary, earning me a glare from Blake.

"Sorry," I mumbled as my hands shook from nervousness whilst I fiddled with my schedule.

We start to stroll towards the school, walking side by side.

"What do you have first hour?" he asks, glancing over my shoulder to read my schedule.

"A.P. English Lit," I say as he opens the door, gesturing for me to go first.

Blake... You never fail to surprise me.

Can you say bipolar?

One second he's an asshole and the next he's holding doors open for me.

"Interesting, me too," he says, leading the way to the class that I'll have to go to every morning for a year.

Sigh.

This is going to be one hell of a year.

When we get to room 203 I start to knock gently on the door, careful not to disturb the class, but then Blake starts banging on it like an idiot. I shoot him a quick glare which brings amusement to his face.

The door swings open making me take a step back in surprise right into Blake, who doesn't move a bit to give me room: so my back is pressed firmly against his front. The teacher, Mrs. Bullock - according to the schedule - sends us both a glare but she doesn't say anything; she simply lets us in. I let out a breath and take a step into the classroom.

Heads turn in our direction and most people look shocked while others look puzzled. There's only two seats left in the back of the class and I sigh as I realize that's where I'm going to have to sit, with Blake.

People watch as we walk to the back of the room and an enormous amount of whispers erupt from the class.

It doesn't take a genius to know what they're saying.

What is he doing with her?

Why did they come in late together?

Are those two an item or something?

Did they not even have the dignity to wait until class was dismissed?

Well this will probably be the worst year of school ever.

Just because the bad boy is my ride.

Chapter 2

"When are you going to get my car fixed?" I ask Blake in fifth hour, crossing my arms across my chest as I frown at him.

Yes we have to sit next to each other in this class too.

Blake simply rolls his eyes, closing his history book that he'd used to hide his face while he slept during Mr. Addison's lecture. "Look, I'll get it fixed. I said I would and I will so stop asking."

Stop asking?

This is the first time I've asked him even though I've had every class with him so far. Yes, little unlucky me has been dealing with Blake all freaking day. Oh, and that's not the worst of it, since both of our last names start with the letter D, and four out of five of our teachers do alphabetical seating charts, we ended up sitting right by each other in every single class. In home room there isn't a seating chart but since we were both late we had to take the only two vacant seats in the back; right next to each other.

It's tortue, I thought they'd stopped doing seating charts back in elementry school.

"I've only asked you one time," I say, getting frustrated.

After five classes I'm starting to realize that Blake is the biggest ass hole I've ever met.

"One time too many." The bell rings and he stands up, turning his back to me and walking away without another word.

I let out an aggravated sigh before making my way to 6th hour -Art-, and I'm happy to find Blake isn't in this class. My best friend Jasmine is though, and we both let out squeals when we see each other. Jasmine has been my best friend since elementary school. Physically we're different; mentally we're just the same. Jasmine has mocha skin with shoulder length black hair and blonde highlights, she's just under five and a half feet tall, her eyes are a pretty hazel and she has a curvy body. Completely different to my slightly pale skin, ocean blue eyes that I got from my mother and small curves that can't even compare to hers. The only thing we have in common is being short and having black hair, though mine is in the middle of my back, and hers is shoulder length since she always gets haircuts.

"I haven't seen you in forever Boo," She says as we take our seats in the middle of the classroom, directly in front of the board.

"You just saw me a week ago," I tell her with a smile on my face.

She leans across her desk towards me and it makes a creaking noise, her eyes are bucked, "Like I said, I haven't seen you in forever."

I roll my eyes just as the teacher; Mrs. Garcia walks into the classroom. She's a Hispanic woman with long curly black hair and she looks like she's in her early 30s but she's around forty five. Jasmine and I have been taking art since freshman year, so we always have Mrs. Garcia, and boy does she love us. She's the only one, well she's the only teacher that loves Jasmine, who tends to stay in trouble.

"Mrs. G.," Jasmine calls out propping her feet up on the chair of the freshman boy in front of her.

Mrs. Garcia looks up from her papers that she'd just started fumbling with; when she sees us a faint smile shows up on her face. "Well, well, well, and here I thought that I'd gotten rid of you two."

"Nope," Jasmine says popping the 'p', "We'll be here until we graduate, I told you this the first day of freshman year."

"Class," Mrs. Garcia calls out ignoring Jasmine "Today we're going to paint how we feel."

"Does bored count as a feeling?" I ask the question that I've asked everyday on the first day of school when we receive this assignment.

"The answer to that is still no, and forever will be no," Mrs. Garcia shakes her head as she starts pulling out art equipment from her cabinets. "Pick an easel in the back and I'll start passing out the supplies."

"Come on," Jasmine says standing up and grabbing hold of my wrist to pull me to the back of the classroom. She stops walking when we get to the easels on the back row that we used last year. Jasmine decided that back here it's harder for her to get caught texting on her phone and she can draw whatever she wants without Mrs. Garcia seeing. I'm pretty sure Mrs. Garcia wouldn't take her phone if she got caught though, she'd probably yell but that's about it.

"Okay class take your time," Mrs. Garcia says as she starts to pass out paintbrushes "I'm not expecting a masterpiece," she looks in our direction with a glare on her face, but it's a friendly one, "But I don't want a picture of a stick figure eating chicken or ice cream."

Jasmine and I giggle at the memory from freshman year when we drew the pictures of stick figures eating. "We felt hungry Mrs. G.," Jasmine says causing Mrs. Garcia to roll her eyes.

"What are you going to draw?" Jasmine asks me as I start wetting my brushes.

"Me shoving a knife through Blake Drayton," I shoot her a smirk.

"About that, what's going on with you guys?" She asks me with a knowing smile on her face "I heard you two are dating. Which upsets me because I thought you would've told me if you were tapping that hot piece of ass."

You've got to be kidding me; I knew the rumors would start but dating? Come on!

He gave me a ride so that means we're dating?

"Of course not," I cringe my nose and frown at her.

"Then what happened?" She starts to move her paintbrush along her easel.

"He hit my car-"

"Oh my god, he hit Antoinette?" Jasmine cuts me off turning to look at me and forgetting about her painting.

"Yea," I don't mention that it was my fault, that part's not important anyway, "So he drove me to school, we had no other options," I dip my brush in red paint knowing exactly what I'm going to draw.

"Oh, so when are you going to get Net fixed?"

Yes, my car has a nickname.

"Blake's supposed to be getting her fixed," I tell her taking out the black paint.

"You know what this means right?" I can hear the slyness in her voice so I turn to face her, seeing she has a smirk on her face.

I let out a sigh "What does this mean Jasmine?"

"This means you get to ride with a hot bad ass to school every morning."

"Language, Jasmine!" Mrs. Garcia calls out with a scowl on her face that Jasmine ignores.

"But I don't want to ride with him," I complain turning back to my picture.

Jasmine lets out a snort, "I'm not going to pick you up." She says, rubbing her chin as she stares at her picture which looks like dirt at the moment.

"Why not?" I ask with a frown on my face.

"Because you should ride with Blake, now that I think about it.." she looks at me from head to toe "You two would be perfect for each other." She says with a smirk.

"Would not," I scowl at her and she chuckles.

"Aw, you're heartbroken," Mrs. Garcia says as she looks at my picture of a broken heart. I nod my head in agreement as Jasmine smiles next to me "I'm so sorry Allison; I didn't know you were even in love."

"Of course," I say placing a hand to my chest "I love Antoinette," she frowns at me, "We'll be back together in a couple of weeks though probably."

"I also didn't know that you're..." She trails off, gesturing to me with her eyebrows scrunched together.

What is she getting at?

"I'm what?" I frown at her.

"Gay," She says sounding confused that I didn't know what she was talking about.

What the hell is she talking about I'm gay?

Wait, she thinks Antoinette is my ex-girlfriend who broke my heart....

Aw hell.

Jasmine finds this funny and starts laughing her ass off, "No Mrs. Garcia." I say, sending Jasmine a glare that she ignores "Antoinette is my car..." I try to explain "This guy hit her this morning so I can't drive her right now."

Mrs. Garcia lets out breath, "Oh that clears things up a whole bunch," She waves a dismissive hand "Get to your last class before you're tardy."

I drag a still laughing Jasmine out of the room and head to the gym happy about going to PE; one of my favorite classes. "You have PE this hour right?" I ask Jasmine who has finally stopped her damn laughing.

"Yep," she pops the 'p' as she opens the gym door revealing the gymnasium. The tardy bell rings signalling we've made it to class just on time.

"Come on in Carter and Darling!" Coach Willis calls out to us using our last names. Coach is a middle aged white woman with short brown hair; she's around five foot seven. I don't think she cared for Jaz and I too much in our freshman year until we started playing sports and she realized we're pretty damn useful.

Jaz and I slide into the bleachers by a couple of other juniors who we know pretty well. "Okay," Coach calls out loudly, "Basketball tryouts are next Tuesday and Wednesday," she passes the permission slips to a freshman who's sitting on the bottom bleacher so she can pass them around. "Soccer tryouts are Thursday and Friday." She passes those permission slips around also.

Yes! This is the reason that I get up every morning and drag my lazy ass to school; for sports. I don't really think that I need to come to school to learn, I'm already smart enough. I could drop out of school now and get my GED if I wanted too. I'm serious, I took a practice test just for the hell of it and I passed it with flying colors. Unfortunately, not many people are willing to recruit a sixteen year old who dropped out of school and got her GED. I could've been skipped up a couple of grades but I don't want to be in a grade with people who are two years older than me. Jaz is smart enough to get skipped up also but I can't say that for the rest of my friends and I don't want to leave them.

"Coach I think I have a date after school on that day!" Jasmine calls out to Coach Willis as we take a slip from each stack.

Coach looks at the part of the bleachers where we're seated, "On which day?" Coach asks her with a frown on her face.

"All of them," Jasmine smirks at her and coach shakes her head.

"Cancel them, I need you at tryouts." She says in a tone letting Jasmine know that her decision is final. Ah yes, did I mention coach thinks she's our second mom? Well, that's exactly how she acts, if we get in trouble not only will we have to run extra laps, but we get a long stern talk after cleaning the whole gym. Including the boy's locker room, and I must say that boys are gross pigs.

"Yes mom," Jasmine rolls her eyes just as the boys on the other half of the gym start laughing as loud as they can.

"This is a rich school yet all we have is one damn gym," I say shaking my head, irritated that I have to spend another year in a gym with a bunch of obnoxious guys. I'm sorry but I believe that there's only one thing boys can do for me. Make Out. Okay, so maybe I'm a bit of a player, not a whore but a player. I have never gone further than making out.

Virgin Pride!

"So girls we're not going to do much today, it's more of a free day, since it's only the first day. If you want to sit in the bleachers I don't care, you can play basketball at one of the goals." She points to the six goals in the gym; three on each end. "Darling, go get some balls out of my office," She says throwing her keys to me.

"Alright," I jog to her office, unlocking the door and pulling some basketballs out of her closet and bringing them back out. Turns out Jaz and I are the only ones who actually want to play a real game. Some girls want to just shoot, some want to dribble around the outside of the court, while others bitch about having PMS so they don't want to play.

"Dammit," I say getting aggravated.

"Well we can play one on one," Jasmine says dribbling a basketball between her legs.

"Okay," I say knocking the ball out of her hands since she isn't expecting it, and I then drive to the goal making a bucket easily. "Ha," I say doing a victory dance with the ball under my arm. "Your ball," I bounce pass the ball to her and she dribbles slowly walking towards me. I hold my hands out and she smirks faking towards her left before driving to my right side easily making a layup.

"Hey we need the court," An arrogant voice calls out, and I turn around to see Blake and some other guys watching us.

"Hell no," I call down the court, pissed that I even have the last class of the day with Blake "Use that half of the court." I cross my arms showing I won't back down.

Blake marches over to where Jaz and I stand with a couple of his minions in tow. "Look here Darling," This earns an eye roll from me, "why don't you and your friend go shoot on one of the side goals and leave the court to people who can actually play." He smirks at me and I want to punch him in his face.

"Why don't we let them play with us?" Daniel Trejings asks, and I decide I like him better than Blake. Daniel is one of the school's hottest guys with short blonde hair and dark blue eyes. Must I say his body is to die for.

"Because they don't know how to play," Blake says and I want to kick his ass even more.

"We should at least let them try," Daniel argues before I can say something that'll end me up in detention.

Blake looks us over, his eyes stopping on mine and he smirks, "Fine." He turns to walk back down the court, "But they're on your team Danny!"

"Drive it Allison!" One of my team members calls to me, completely ignoring the fact that Blake is standing his tall ass in front of me so I can't shoot or drive. Seeing Jaz open, I pass her the ball and she heads towards the goal. I V-Cut Blake to get rid of him before cutting through the lane and recieving a pass from Jasmine. I do a jump shot and make it.

"That's what I'm talking about," Daniel calls out clapping his hands which seems to make Blake mad. He snatches the ball off the ground as his team takes the ball out.

I wait for Blake at half-court as he plays point guard and brings the ball down the court. As soon as he gets to the half-court line I start pressuring him and I don't let up until he passes the ball which Jasmine intercepts. I sprint to the other side of the court filling the lane trying to do a fast break, and she passes the ball to me. Just as I go in for the layup I'm knocked on my ass.

What the hell?

I look up to see Blake with the ball heading back down the court.

Oh no he doesn't!

I get up and run full speed down the court bumping Blake hard with my hip and stealing the ball back. If he's going to treat me like a man I'm sure as hell going to play like one.

"Good job Allison," A guy says to me on my way out of the gym and I smile at him.

"You better play just like that this season," Coach tells me in a stern voice but I can see the slight smile on her face.

"You know I am," I say "Assuming I make the team." We both know I'm going to make it but it only seems fair to act oblivious.

Jasmine jogs up to me with a smile on her face and we do our special handshake, "We kicked ass my sister," she pats me on the back, "Now I have to go home and get ready for my date."

I shake my head at her watching as she jogs over to her car and leaves. I pull my keys out of my pocket, hitting the unlock button and frowning when I don't hear Antoinette make a beep.

What the hell?

Shit, I completely forgot about Blake driving me to school this morning.

I look around and see Blake standing by his car talking to a couple of guys. I hold my head up and walk towards him fully aware of my shirt sticking to my body since I'm covered in sweat.

The guys turn to watch as I walk over to them, Blake's the only one paying me no attention. He continues to talk and I cross my arms glaring at him.

Finally Blake looks at me as if he didn't know I was staring at him "Yes?" He asks raising a brow in annoyance.

What a freaking jerk!

"I need a ride," I say sounding annoyed myself.

"Yea, yea, yea," he says, waving a dismissive hand before pointing a finger at his car, "Get in." He then turns around and starts back talking, though most of the guys' eyes are still on me, especially as I turn my backside to them as I walk around the car.

I get in the passenger seat slamming the door and crossing my arms over my chest. Dammit, my butt hurts because of that asshole. Now I'm going to have to sit in an hour bath of hot water and Epson salt. I look at my watch, oh my goodness will he bring his ass on? It's too damn hot in this car, he could've at least given me the keys to turn the air on.

Finally, Blake gets in the car slowly, still laughing and talking with the guys who are trying to get a peek at me. "Alright guys, I'll talk to you tomorrow." He says before closing his door and starting the car.

"Took long enough," I mutter under my breath.

"What was that?" He glances at me and I shake my head looking out the window.

I give Blake the directions to my house, unhappy to see my mom sitting on the porch with some man. I'm not really bothered by seeing the man sitting on the porch but I know my mom is going to question me about Blake. I'm proved right when she squints her eyes at the car before starting to walk over.

"Oh hell," I say banging my head against the dashboard, "Shit," I say rubbing my forehead before looking to my left to see an amused Blake. "What?" I groan out.

"Just found you hitting your head against something funny since I've been wishing for it all day." He tells me with a crooked smile.

I glare at him opening my mouth to say something, but a knock on the driver's window stops me. Blake lets down the window and my mom pokes her head in, "Where's your car?" She asks me bluntly completely ignoring Blake.

"On the side of the road," I say and she narrows her eyes at me.

"Who are you?" She turns her gaze on Blake now and I sigh slipping out of the car while my mom interrogates him.

I walk past my mom's "guest" and go inside the house, upstairs to my room and sit down at my desk.

Today has been one long day. Antoinette's on the side of the road, I have to deal with a jerk all freaking day. And to top it off my ass hurts.

Chapter 3

When I wake up I feel like crap and my butt is in agony. I stand up, wiping the sleep out of my eyes and stumbling over to my closet. I pull out a pair of khaki cargos and a light blue tank top, deciding I'll just dress comfortably. After brushing my teeth, washing my face, and changing, I jog down the stairs.

I find my mother in the same spot she was in yesterday and yet again she's eating an apple. Instead of reading the newspaper though she's reading a magazine. When she sees me enter she closes it. "I'm going to contact Blake's mom today about getting your car fixed." She narrows her eyes at me and I wonder what Blake told her.

"'Okay," I say with a shrug, opening the refrigerator door and looking for something quick to eat. "Mom, you really need to go grocery shopping," I complain, closing the door and grabbing a bag of chips to eat out of the snack jar.

"I'm not the one who's hungry," she says, going back to her magazine.

Best mother ever, right? Note the sarcasm.

I walk outside slamming the kitchen door behind me. It finally dawns on me that I have no ride to school. Shit.

I'm just about to pull out my phone to call Jasmine when I see a Ferrari sitting in the driveway. Well, maybe he isn't that bad of a person.

The driver's side window rolls down and Blake sticks his head out. "Hurry up I don't have all damn day." He rolls his window back up.

Okay, I was so wrong. He's still a freaking jerk.

I stomp over to the passenger's side, swinging the door open and slamming it shut, ignoring the glare I receive from Blake. His radio is blasting some dumbass rap song and it starts to irritate me so I change it.

"Don't touch my shit," he says, changing the radio from a Ke$ha song that was just playing.

Does he really have to cuss in every sentence? My goodness, he's worse than me and Jasmine combined.

I change the station back to what I was listening to. "I'll touch your shit all I want." I seriously don't see why girls fall at his feet - he's so damn rude and annoying.

"I'm going to put you out of my car," he threatens, shooting me daggers with his eyes.

"And I'll slash all your tires," I fire back, knowing that with Jasmine's help I could make it happen by lunchtime.

"You're so annoying." He turns his eyes back to the road leaving the radio alone.

"That's like the pot calling the kettle black." I smirk, knowing I've won this argument.

One point for Darling, zero for Drayton.

"He picked you up this morning?" Jasmine asks, raising a brow at me from across the lunch table with a wicked smile on her face.

"Who picked you up this morning?" My best guy friend - David - asks, coming up to the table.

David and I have been best friends since the sixth grade but we met in the third grade. You used to not be able to stick us in a room together for more than thirty seconds or there would be war.

David is the ultimate player - although he doesn't have Blake beat - and he has no morals when it comes to girls. He was a freaking bully in elementary school, always picking on people. He also lived right across the street from me. Anyway, he didn't like the fact that I wouldn't take his crap like the other girls. We always ended up fighting - both physically and verbally.'

One day in fourth grade when we were waiting in line to go to the gym he threw paper in my face - for no freaking reason - and I pushed him into a desk. Also, we're both very competitive and we were the smartest kids in our grade so we were always duking it out when it came to academics.

Things changed when we went to middle school. All of our classes - mostly honors - were filled with people we didn't know. Snobby people. We then started making jokes and talking about them every day - that was the start of our friendship. Now David and I are like brother and sister, we tell each other everything. Well, he tells me about how far he's gone with his flings even when I tell him to stop, and trust me, he's very detailed.

"Blake," Jasmine says, shoving a fry in her mouth.

"Drayton?" David questions, sitting next to me and running a hand through his curly brown hair that matches his caramel skin he inherited from being biracial.

"Yes," I say with a sigh. "I told you we got into a wreck, right?" I can't remember if I mentioned it to him yesterday or not.

"Yep, Jaz told me." He licks one of his fingers and sticks his hand on Jasmine's pizza. "You're not going to eat that, are you?" He smirks at her.

Jasmine narrows her eyes at him. "There's no telling how many STD's you have." He starts to reach for the pizza but Jasmine pours milk all over it. "Doesn't mean you get to have it." She smirks at him grabbing her backpack. "See y'all later." She stalks off towards a group of boys who all stare at her.

"She gets on my nerves," he grunts out before turning towards me. "Man, Allison." He starts to grin again.

Uh oh, this isn't going to be good.

"You know Lexi, right?" - His current girlfriend, if I'm not mistaken - "She looks sweet but I promise you she's a freak."

"And this is where I leave you," I tell him, grabbing my things and scurrying off towards class.

I walk in and see Blake by our desks talking to a group of girls.

Maybe I should've stayed at the lunch table with David. It would've been better than this.

I walk over to my desk, shoving a couple of blondes out of my way. They glare at me but I simply flip them off. They leave and walk over to their desk across the room.

When I bend over to reach into my backpack I see Blake staring at me - not in a checking-me-out way either. "What?" I snap, placing my notebooks on my table.

"Do you always have to ruin all my fucking fun?" He sighs, slipping into his seat next to mine.

"Do you always have to curse?" I tilt my head to the side, smirking at him as annoyance runs across his face loud and clear.

Well maybe this isn't so bad; it seems I get under his skin. A lot.

"Okay class," Mrs. Franklin walks in, interrupting Blake before he can say anything.

"I would drive you home but I rode with Brandon this morning," Jasmine says with an apologetic look on her face after school. "Ask David."

"He's taking Lexi home and I'd rather not witness live porn in a cramped car," I say with a sigh, glancing across the parking lot to see Blake chatting away with his friends just like yesterday.

"I'm sorry," Jasmine apologizes again.

"It's fine," I tell her, running a hand through my hair, "I'm just going to have to suck up my pride and ride with that asshole." I wave at her before walking towards Blake's car.

Again all the boys start staring at me as if I'm the last piece of candy in the candy shop and they're a bunch of little kids. Blake doesn't even bother glancing in my direction; he just continues to talk as if he hasn't noticed me.

I highly doubt that since all of his friends are staring at me.

I simply walk past them to the passenger seat and get in without saying a word. I dare Blake to try to make me get out. I swear I'll cut off his family jewels and make him drive me to my house before he goes to the hospital for help.

The driver's door opens and Blake gets in the car not looking at me.

Ha, I guess he's realized who runs things around here.

"You know, it is polite to ask people for a ride instead of just hopping into their car," he finally says to me half way to my house.

"Like you know how to be polite." I snort at the thought.

"If I weren't polite I wouldn't have offered to get your car fixed even though it was your fault we wrecked it in the first place. I also wouldn't have given you a ride to school."

"Whatever," I say, rolling my eyes, knowing he has me beat.

I'm surprised to see another woman sitting on the porch with my mother. She tends to have more male visitors than female ones.

"Who's that?" I ask, squinting my eyes, noticing the woman is quite lovely with wavy brown hair and clover green eyes.

"My mom," Blake says, surprising me as he turns his car off and follows me up the driveway.

"Oh, how nice that you're both here," my mother says giggling as we follow her into the house. She's completely wasted. This is definitely not good.

"Why is that nice?" I ask sceptically.

"Because we have news," she says, gesturing between her and Blake's mother who is sitting at the table rolling a lemon around and grinning like an idiot.

For how freaking long have they been drinking?

"We use to be best friends in high school," Blake's mother says, forgetting about her lemon for a second.

"Okay?" Blake says with a confused look on his face.

"That's not the news though." She goes back to playing with her lemon.

"Nope," my mother says, popping the 'p'. "The news is that, to teach you two responsibility, we're not going to get your car fixed, Allison."

What the hell?

"You two are going to be riding to school together until we feel you're responsible enough to get your car back."

Aw, shit.

"Exciting, huh?" My mother takes a swig of something I'm sure isn't tea and she starts to giggle again. "You're going to be car-pooling buddies from now on."

Chapter 4

"Stop looking at me like that," Blake says as I get into his car which makes my scowl deepen," Look," He pulls out of the driveway quickly, "It's not like I enjoy us riding together either." He says.

I really don't care about what he says if he wouldn't have given my mom his mom's number we wouldn't be in this situation; Or if he would've stopped his car when he saw me run the stupid stop sign. Its been two days since they declared we have to ride to school together and its making me grumpier as the days go by.

"I don't want to hear it," I mutter looking out the window which makes me notice he isn't going in the direction of the school.

"Where are you going, school's back that way," I point my finger over my shoulder pointing to the way that leads to the school.

"Yea, I've been going to Legacy for three years I know where it is," He says sarcastically rolling his eyes.

"Then why in the hell aren't you going in that direction," I ask anger radiating off of me.

It doesn't help that my mom pissed me off this morning so I was already in a bad mood when I got into the car. Yesterday instead of riding with Blake I rode with Jasmine which I planned on doing until Antoinette gets fixed, but no mom just isn't going to let that happen. So this morning my mom totally bitched me out. I mean why is it so important for me to ride

with this stupid bastard. Okay he may not be stupid considering he has
A.P. classes.

"We have to go pick someone up," He says turning onto a street that
I've never been on before, "You're not the only person I have to pick up
Sweetcheeks."

Sweetcheeks? Ugh, I hate him.

"Don't call me that," I mutter crossing my arms across my chest and I see
him smirk from the corner of my eye.

He pulls the car into a driveway that's attatched to a two-story house
with big windows everywhere that have black curtains drawn from the
inside.

Blake honks his horn and the front door of the house opens, a guy walks
out with his head hanging down as he looks at his phone. He doesn't even
look up when he gets to the door simply opens it and goes to sit down.

The shriek that escapes me is ear piercing and the boy jumps almost
dropping his phone, "Watch where you're going!" I yell hearing Blake in
the background laughing like he's just seen the funniest thing in history.

The guy looks at me with a death glare before a smirk appears on his face,
"Well hello there," He tries to put on his charm but despite the fact that
he's hot with his blonde hair, hazel eyes, and nice build, I ain't falling for
it.

"I don't have time for you to sit here and try to flirt with me, I need to
get to school," I say narrowing my eyes at him, "So get your ass in the car."

He glares at me before muttering something under his breath and getting in the backseat. Blake is still laughing and when I glare at him it
doesn't subside one bit. Finally he starts to back out of the driveway and
his laughing is only a bright smile on his face now.

When we get to school I finally notice that we weren't riding in the Ferrari but a BMW. What the hell? This boy has a Ferrari and a BMW, those are expensive ass cars.

"See you in first hour SweetCheeks," Blake says to me as we get out of the car and I glare at him which simply makes him laugh.

I storm over to Jasmine who's hanging out with a bunch of guys. No surprise there.

"Hey Allison," Ryan Freeman says smiling at me showing perfect white teeth. Ryan Freeman is a hottie with flawless light brown hair, light brown eyes, and olive skin and any other day that I would flirt with him, but not today.

I simply wave a hand to let him know I heard him and I hear all the boys teasing him as I walk away about my diss.

"You just totally blew Ryan off," Jasmine says looking at me in amusement, "Why?" Before I can answer her she looks at my shoulder "Hotties at 6 'oclock."

I turn around and see Blake, the phone guys, and two more boys talking to a bunch of girls who all look fake.

"Uh," I say rolling my eyes at her, "That bastard is definitely not hot."

Jasmine glares at me, "You know damn well every single guy over there is hot, including Blake even if you think he's an asshole." She says knowing she's right.

"I really don't care," I cross my arms poking my lip out, "Him and Blondie both are jerks, so I don't give a damn how much of a sharpie either one of them are."

What's a sharpie you ask. Well a sharpie is a boy who is definitely a "20.5" -or higher- on a scale from 1-10. Jasmie and I came up with the word when we were in middle school and became more interested in boys.

"The blond?" Jasmine raises a brown squinting her eyes as she looks at the group, she turns back to me "You mean Will?"

"I guess, I have no idea what his name is and I don't care."

She smirks, "Well I know his name pretty well."

"Jasmine, that's so gross," I frown scrunching my face up.

"I'm joking," She says with a big smile on her face,"I had calculus with him, trust me," She holds up her hands, "I'm not interested in touching that he probably has more STDs than a hooker who doesn't use protection."

"So basically he has more STDs than you?" I smirk at her already in a better mood.

"Yeap," She says smirking back at me which makes me laugh. This is why Jasmine and I are best friends, she's amazing.

"Hey, why aren't you in A.P. classes?" I suddenly ask remembering that she isn't in A.P. classes as usual.

"The office screwed up my schedule and I'm on a waiting list," She scoffs, "But when my mom calls up here she'll get that bitch of a secretary to stop screwing around and wasting my time." She shakes her head, "I do plan on getting into Harvard and I'm not going to get accepted with regular classes."

Jasmine plans on getting an acceptance letter from Harvard but she doesn't plan on going there. Hell, with her grades and smartness I'm pretty sure she can get into any college she wants.

"I'll see you at lunch," Jasmine says as she drops me off at first hour, "Don't do anything I would do between now and then." She winks at me and I chuckle before walking into the classroom.

I take my seat next to Blake a deep scowl coming onto my face when I see Will sitting next to him. This class was just full the other day, and how is this dumb ass in A.P. I look around the class noticing there are a couple of empty seats now. I would move to one of them but people have decided to put their stupid backpacks in those seats.

"Well look who it is," Will says leaning over Blake to get a good look at me.

I roll my eyes ignoring him as I get out a book from my bag. Out of the corner of my eye I see Will lean back in his seat and start playing on his phone.

"What'cha reading?" Blake looks over my shoulder to look at my book. I can tell he's just trying to annoy me as usual. I don't reply simply continue to read, "From what I've heard about you, you don't seem like the type to read books." He starts to tap his fingers on my desk.

"Stop that," I say after he continues to tap on my desk for a couple of minutes.

"Ouch," He says when I smack his hand away from my desk.

"I told you to stop," I hiss at him closing my book as the teacher walks into the room with a grinning Jasmine.

Jasmine smiles at me walking towards my seat, she turns to the girl sitting next to me and sends her a harsh glare, "Move." She says and the girl quickly grabs her things and moves to a different seat.

"How did you get in so quickly?" I ask her.

"Mom called and had a good discussion with the secretary," She says with a sly smile.

Jasmine's mom -Ada- is hilarious and stubborn as hell, just like Jasmmine. I have no doubt that she cussed out the secretary and threatened her. She doesn't like when someone is bothering any of her children, so I'm pretty sure she was pissed about Jasmine not having A.P. when she qualified. Don't get me wrong Ada can be sweet and is very nice but she doesn't like when people "effing around with her", which is actually the clean version of what she actually said.

"Oh, I love your mom," I say and we both giggle. All of a sudden Jasmine smirks,"What?" She nods over my shoulder and I turn to see Will and Blake playing on both of their phones.

"I'm even happier now about my classes getting changed," She says and I roll my eyes.

"OKay, class we're going to be doing a group project," The teacher says, her screechy voices echoing around the class cutting through all the noise."You're going to have to shoot a commercial.." She goes on about what the projects about and I ignore her until she starts to split groups up.

"You four," She points to Me, Jasmine, Blake, and WIll.

Oh hell naw.

"Watch your mouth in my class Mrs. Darling!" She suddenly yells at me.

Well, I guess I didn't say that inside of my head.

Jasmine bursts out into fits of laughter which earns her a glare from the teacher but she ignores her. Finally, she stops laughing and walks up to the teacher's desk to get our project packet.

"Well, this should be entertaining," Jasmine says sitting at her desk.

"No! No!" Jasmine yells thumping Will on the forehead, "That isn't right you dumbass!" She starts to erase whatever he wrote down on the paper "My name is spelled J-A-S-M-I-N-E, not J-A-Z-M-E-N."

So right now me, Jasmine, Will, and Blake are at my house working on this stupid project. We have to start working on it now before Jasmine and I have to start basketball and soccer practice.

I laugh as Will glares at Jasmine who flicks him in the forehead again, "You bitch!" Will says rubbing his forehead.

Oh, why did he just call her a bitch?

"Who are you calling a bitch, I am not a bitch you jackass..."

I leave out of the room and walk into the kitchen grabbing lemonade out of the icebox. We've been trying to work on this project for the last hour but haven't gotten anywhere at all. Will and Jasmine keep finding things to argue about. Blake has been getting calls from different girls every five freaking minutes, while I have been trying to get some work done on the project. I'm pretty sure we're not gonna get past writing our names down on the paper.

If we get past that.

After pouring a cup of lemonade for myself I sit down at the table and start playing on my phone.

"Shouldn't we be working on the project?" I jump out of my seat at the sound of Blake's voice. I almost waste lemonade all over myself but somehow I managed not to drop it, I did drop my phone though.

"I was trying," I say bending down to pick up my phone, "But it seems I'm working with two five year olds, and a man-whore so I gave up." I sit back up and notice my lemonade isn't on the table anymore.

Blake smirks as he sits my now empty glass of lemonade on the table wiping his mouth with the sleeve of his shirt.

That asshole drunk my lemonade.

"Is someone jealous about all those girls calling me," He sits down across from me with amusement in his eyes, "Don't worry SweetCheeks they can't compete with you." He winks at me and I feel myself blush, "Aww," He says in a teasing tone, "the blush of a virgin is the best."

I stand up turning my back to him as I grab another cup from the cabinet and get the lemonade out of the fridge. I feel a presence behind me and I tense up knowing its Blake.

Dammit, dammit, dammit. Alison don't let him think he's getting to you, I warn my self.

His minty breath brushes against my neck and he puts both of his hands on either side of me against the counter trapping me. "It's so rude to turn your back on company," He says softly.

What is he doing?

Nope, the better question is what is he doing to me?

I turn around so that I'm facing him and I tilt my head back to look him in the eyes. Those sure are a gorgeous shade of green.

Snap out of it Allison, we have a resistance to his charm.

Blake leans down close to my face and rubs his face against my neck making me shiver.

Why am I not making him stop?

I'm just about to push him away but he moves his lips close to my ear and I've lost all resistance that I had.

He suddenly leans away with a smirk on his face, "Pour me a glass would you?" He holds out a cup to me.

Chapter 5

I let out a frustrated sigh into my pillow. It's been a got damn week and I still can't get what happened with Blake off of my mind. That sick bastard knew what he was doing, going and getting me all flustered and then he asks me to refill his cup, which was actually my cup by the way.

A knock at my door interrupts my sigh, "Come in!" I call out rolling over to look at my door as it opens.

My mom walks in with a short black dress on. What the hell? I raise an eyebrow at her taking in her whole appearance. Web my mom wears makeup it's barely noticeable but tonight she looks like a bratz doll.

"Mom why are you dressed like that?" I ask her sitting up on the bed making it creak beneath me.

"It's really none of your business," She states crossing her arms over her chest, "but if you must know I'm going out with Beatrice." She informs me.

Oh no. Every since the stupid accident her and Beatrice -Blake's mom- have been going out almost every day. I should've known without even asking.

"Where to?" I ask with a sigh.

My mother scowls at me, "To Yeldarado."

Let out yet another sigh. Yeldarado is the most boo leg place. It's part casino, part bar, part restraunt, part strip club, and it's all in the same room. I mean come on, who wants to east and drink while looking at some strippers goodies being flaunt every where. gross.

I rub my forehead in frustration, "Okay mom," I shake my head knowing there's no point in arguing with her.

My mom smiles before heading out of the door, "Oh," She turns around to look at me, "Someone's coming to keep you company." She closes my bedroom door before I can ask who's coming over.

I'm in the middle of rereading "Twilight" when my doorbell ring. I let out an aggravated grunt before going to answer the door. Without checking the peephole I swing the door open.

My eyes land on a tight fitted t-shirt with obvious tone muscles underneath. I tip my head back coming face to face with Blake.

"Go home," I say trying to close the door on him.

Blake's foot shoots out stopping me from closing the door, "Nu uh Sweetcheeks, I'm your baby sitter for the night." He winks before pushing the door opening, stepping around me, and walking towards the living room.

"Where's the Tv?" He asks with a frown on his face when I walk into the room.

"In the bedrooms," I say scrunching my eyebrows together.

He starts heading towards the stairs before I can react. I follow him and notice he stops at my bedroom door, which has soccer and basketball stickers on it.

"Hey what are you doing!" I yell as he casually walks into my room plopping down on the bed with his hands behind his head.

"Where's the remote?" He asks looking around the room ignoring my question. His eyes light up as soon as they land on the remote.

Before he can even move to grab it I snatch it off the nightstand. "Not so fast," I say crossing my arms over my chest, remote still in my hand.

Blake frown sticking out his bottom lip slightly. He looks just as cute as a puppy, and I love puppies. I'm not suppose to be thinking about how cute he is, I remind my self.

"Get out!" I point a finger at my door.

"No can do Sweetcheeks," He says sitting up on the bed.

"Stop calling me that," I say deepening my frown.

"Look Sweetcheeks," He says totally ignoring my request, "Its seven, meaning your making me miss Bad Girls Club."

I simply stare at him in shock.

"What?" He scrunched up his nose studying my face, "I'm a guy and they are always flashing their asses or having fights in their underwear, that's a total turn on."

You've got to be freaking kidding me

"Your making me miss hot ass," He says in a pouting tone before a smirk appears on his face, as he looks at me expectantly, "Unless your going to show me yours."

Before I can even think twice I've tackled him onto the bed.

Blake simply laughs before flipping us over putting me underneath him. He grabs my arms pinning them above my head with one hand, "Now that was a bad idea Darling."

There's a glint of something in his eyes that I can quite place. He smiles as he leans in towards my neck.

Hell no, we are not about to have another repeat of last time.

"You know Sweetcheeks," His husky voice whispers in my ear causing a shiver to escape me, "I think Bad Girl's Club can wait." He says before kissing my neck ever so lightly.

Don't go lower, I think to myself knowing he's getting close to my weak spot. My body starts to heat up anticipating his next move. His lips start to trail lower down my neck.

Crap.

I have to stop this.

I attempt to flip us over before he can reach my weak spot. It doesn't work successfully and we both end up on the floor.

Blake swears from underneath me pushing me off of him ungently. I land with an "oomph" on the ground. I stand up rubbing my now hurting bottom. Damn, what is it with him always making me land on my butt.

Blake stands up with an un pleased frown, swiftly grabbing the remote from where I dropped it. He plops down on my bed hitting the power button on the remote.

I feel slightly dizzy, and I'm burning up, without saying a word walk out of my room.

When I firs met Blake I felt nothing what's so ever despite all the undying gossip about how hot he is. Of course I noticed how hot he is, but I really didn't care. The only thing I felt was anger since he hit Antoinette. Look at me now though, feeling all flustered and all he did was kiss my neck. Maybe it's because I haven't had a good hookup in a while. Yep, that's definatelty it. Looks like I'm going to have to fix that.

After rinsing my face with cold water, I walk back into my room grabbing my phone off the charger. I try not to look at Blake (Who's frowning and watching Bad girls club) as I scroll through my contacts. I see Tyler's name and a wicked smile appears on my face.

Me: Hey Ty R U busy??

His Reply comes with a couple of seconds.

Ty: Not If you need me..

I glance over at Blake before typing in a message.

Me: How about you come pick me up?

Ty: Be there in a sec.

Me: Don't bother honking your horn R ringing the doorbell, I'll be waiting on the porch outside.

I slip my phone in my pocket glancing at Blake. "I'm going to get something from the kitchen," I say telling him a lie of the back of my head. I don't even know why I bother since he doesn't even reply, simply continues to frown at the TV.

I slip out of the house closing the door quietly. When Tyler pulls up I sprint to his truck opening the passenger door.

"Hey babe," Tyler says flipping his blonde hair as he looks at me with a smile.

"Hey," I say as he pulls out of my driveway with one arm around the back of my seat.

"So," He looks at me with his blue eyes, "My house?"

I nod knowing tonight is going to be fun, and it's going to take care of my Blake problem.

I walk into my house knowing my mom isn't home since her car wasn't in the driveway. I hum as I grab some snacks out of the kitchen. I'm perfectly sure I just had the best make out session of my life. Of course I didn't do the nasty with Tyler or anything but we weren't far from it.

When I walk into my room my smile instantly drops from my face when I see Blake sitting on my bed glaring at me.

Damn.

Chapter 6

S hit.

Shit.

Shit.

"Where were you?" Blake asks interrupting my 'shit' trauma, with his arms folded over his chest as he glares at me.

Think Allison.

"Uh, I lost my way to the kitchen," I say nervously running a hand through my hair. I mentally slap my forehead knowing the lie I came up with is just plain stupid.

"Do you really think I believe that," He narrows is eyes at me, "Try again."

I rub my forehead "Uh.." I draw out, "I went for a walk." So this lie isn't good still but it's an improvement.

Blake takes steps towards me and I back up until my back hits the wall, he doesn't stop until his body impressed against mine. I can feel his minty breath fanning my face and I almost faint.

Oh no, I'm not suppose to be affected by him sill, I'm suppose to be cured. Shit.

Blake grabs a piece of my black hair twirling it around his tan index finger, "Now," he says looking down at me gently pulling my hair, "Are you going to tell me the truth, or are you going to lie all night." He tilts his head to the side slightly as he studies me.

"I may have went out," I admit finally telling some of the truth.

"Mmm hmm," he continues to twirl my hair looking at me expectantly, waiting for the rest of my story, "Where did you go out to?" He asks.

The last time I checked he was mad at me, now he's playing with my hair and asking where I've been.

Again he has me thinking he's bipolar.

"A friend's house," I say being as unclear as possible.

"What friend?" He narrows his eyes at me once again, going back to being a meanie.

"Tyler," I say so low it's almost a whisper.

He stops twirling my hair, "Who?" He asks in a hard tone.

"Tyler," I say a little louder.

He studies me for a second takin n my whole body making me feel nervous again. His eyes trail up and they sop on my neck. If even possible his eyes harden even more. He lets go of my hair brushing his finger over the side of my neck.

Shit.

"And I'm guessing he gave you this right?" He pokes my neck and I know exactly what he's talking about.

It's not none of his business so I have no idea why he cares.

"Maybe he did," I say standing up taller looking at him, trying to stand my ground, "Why does it matter to you anyway?" I ask.

His eyes soften and his body relaxes a bit but its obvious that he's tense, "It doesn't." He says backing away from me but his eyes are still locked with mine, "I was just wondering where you were, I mean wouldn't it make me a bad babysitter if I didn't." He tries to lessen the tension and it works.

I break eye contact as I scowl at him, "You are not my babysitter."

He chuckles as he lays back on my bed with his hands behind his head. "You missed a opulent of good fight on the Bad Girls Club." He informs me.

I roll my eyes going over to my vanity and sitting on the stool. I look in the mirror as I braid my hair, the hickey on my neck sticks out and I cringe. I must look like a tramp to Blake, going out in the middle of the night and hooking up with some guy. If only he knew he reason behind what I did, and the crap still didn't even work.

I let up a sigh and glance at my bed to see Blake casually texting. He looks up from his phone at me with those pretty clover eyes. "Next time you should tell me before you go and run off." He informs me and I roll my eyes.

After I'm done with my braid I grab some pajamas going in the bath-room to change. When I come back into my room Blake isn't texting anymore, instead he's scrolling through the stations on TV.

"Stop!" I yell snatching the remote out of his hand.

He looks at me with big eyes like I just grew a second head, "Damn girl," he says in that husky voice, which is a definite turn on, shit, not again, I can't keep thinking of how man turn ons and crap he has, "What's your problem?" He asks raising a brow at me.

"Twilight's on," I inform him.

"Hell no," he says trying to snatch the remote from my hand, "Twilight is gay."

"Is not," I argue.

"Is too," he fires back still tying to get the remote but I manage to keep it away from him.

"Is not."

"Is to."

"Is not."

"Is too, so shut up," He says finally managing to snatch the remote from me, "Harry Potter is much better." He says changing the station to Harry Potter.

"This is a bunch of crap," I pout, "Everyone dies." I argue.

"It's realistic babe," He says and I scowl at his name for me, "Not everything can be rainbows and unicorns." He turns to me frowning, "Now get
over it and come watch TV with me."

"No."

"Yes."

"No."

"Yes."

We continue to argue like five year olds until we finally agree on The Lion
King.

I frown looking around my room. I'm so not going to lay in the bed with
Blake. I look at my couch and debate on laying on it. It has a nice view of
the TV but the view from the bed is s much better.

"Don't worry Sweetcheeks, I don't bite," Blake says winking at me, "Unless you want me too," he runs his eyes up and down my body licking his
lips.

Sexy. Definitely another turn on. Shit, here we go yet again.

"Perv," I say punching his shoulder.

He grabs my hand pulling me down onto the bed with him. He turns
off the purple lamp on my nightstand before wrapping his arm around m
shoulders and pulling me into him.

Well maybe laying with him for the night won't be too bad. It's not like
we're going to do anything, and for the most part he's being sweet right
now. I relax against him with a sigh resting my head on his shoulder. I feel
as his face turns into a smile as his face moves on the top of my head.

"Don't get too happy." I warn him looking to see that he indeed has a
smile on his face.

"Wouldn't dream of it Sweetcheeks," he says but the smile doesn't leave
his face.

I turn back to the TV with a smile of my own on my face.

"Are you crying?"

"Of ourselves not."

"Yea you are."

"Shut up."

I sit up studying Blake's face and see that he has tears in his eyes. I start laughing "O-oh m-m-my gosh," I stutter holding my stomach as I roar with laughter, "Your crying this is hilarious."

"It's not funny," He says wiping his eyes.

"It totally is," I argue wiping tears from my eyes that came from laughing so hard.

"How can you blame me?" He shrieks, "Mufasa just died." He sits up on the bed glaring at me.

I break out into hysterical laughter once again. He's suppose to be the school's bad oh yet he cries during the Lion King. "This is priceless." I say out loud holding my cheeks which hurt from laughing.

"Are you done?" Blake asks frowning at me.

I hold up a finger signaling for him to give me a second, "Okay," I say taking a deep breath, "I'm done now." I say smiling an actual genuine smile at him.

Blake's eyes soften and he stops glaring at me. He tilts his head to the side before taking a deep breath.

In this second he seems so normal. He's not perving on me, or swearing , he's not even teasing me. He's just sitting hear with me being serious. He leans in towards me and I know he's going to go for my neck.

Soft lips press against mine and I'm so shocked I don't even react. Blake pulls bak a sort of shocked look on his face, he studies my face, but I'm pretty sure he sees nothing but blankness.

"I'm sor-" He starts but I cut him off when I press my lips back against his.

His lips as so soft, I'm pretty sure mines feel like sand paper against his. He grabs my cheek rubbing his thumb across it soothingly. I run my hands through his hair before locking them around his neck. His hands trail to my back before grab my hips, he Gus me to him before flipping me over onto the bed. There are thousands of butterflies in my stomach right now and I seriously wish they would just die.

Blake's fingers make circles on my hips causing me to shiver. We pull back for air, but he cheats and starts to kiss my neck. He goes to the opposite side of where my hikes is from Tyler. He kisses my weak spot softly and my back archs. I feel him smile against my neck as he runs his tongue across it.

Shit, shit, shit.

I'm so far gone right now I simply let him toy with me before pulling his lips back to mine. I flip us over straddling him and roughly kissing him. I hear him let out a moan and I smile.

The smile drops off my face as soon as I hear my mom laughing and talking as she comes up the stairs. Heading towards my room.

Shit.

I roll off of Blake quickly standing up and staring at him with wide eyes. Shit.

"Hey," Blake protests, "What the hell?" He frowns at me before glancing at my door, "Shit."

Yes, my thoughts exactly.

"Get off my bed," I exclaim pushing him off my bed before trying to straighten out my hair. I remember its in a braid so it shouldn't be that wild before stopping.

Blake gets off of my floor rubbing his behind as he makes his way over to my couch, he glares at me the whole time he makes his way to it.

"Sorry," I mutter looking at him with his hair that I messed up, "Fix your hair." I hiss and he runs a hand through it ask that helps.

I roll my eyes siting on my bed just as the door opens.

"Hey kids!" My mom says loudly wobbling her way into my room with her arm around Beatrice's shoulder.

"Hi mom," I say shaking my head at how drunk she is.

She plops down on my bed bringing Beatrice down with her. They basically push me off my bead and I stand up with a scowl. This is ridiculous.

"Did you kids have fun tonight?" Beatrice asks.

I see Blake smirk from the corner of my eye as he stands up, "Yep," He says a bit too happily.

"That's good," My mom says smiling at us.

"Yea, yea, yea, whatever," I say "You need some sleep mom." I tell her pulling her off of my bed and letting her lean against my side.

Blake picks his mom up off my bed. "Looks like you to has fun tonight too." He says wrapping his arm around her shoulder, "Maybe a little too much fun." He shakes his head but amusement is clear in his face.

"See you later Sweetcheeks." Blake says as he walks his mom to the door. He turns around glancing at me and something flashes in his eyes before Beatrice sends me a drunken wave and they leave.

I walk my mom to her room laying her down on her queen size bed. I sigh as she starts spouting crap about a damn cat.

"Alright mom," I say and she sends me a smile before fallen asleep.

I walk back to my room hopping in bed. Tonight was a long night. Turns out I have the Blake disease (not able to resist Blake), Blake's kisses are way better than Tyler's, he cries during the Lion King, and 'shit' is my favorite word while around him.

Chapter 7

"Why do you look like a zombie?" Jasmine asks poking my eyes - which have bags under them. "No, you look more like a raccoon," she decides still poking and prodding at my face.

"Will you stop that?" I ask slapping her hands away from my face.

"Ouch," she says holding her hand like I really hurt her.

"Oh, stop pouting," I say as we make our way into the classroom. I sit in my desk laying my head down.

"You're the one pouting," she mutters. "So," she draws out and I feel her start to mess with my hair. "Do you look like a zombie-raccoon because of a certain person named Blake who you tried your best to avoid this morning?"

I turn my head to face her seeing that she has a mischievous smile on her face. "Why are you looking like that?" I question her.

"Stop avoiding the question," she says shaking her finger at me.

"I'm not avoiding anything," I inform her as a couple of loud students walk in just about drowning our conversation out.

"Oh yea?" she says raising a brow, "Then why haven't you answered the question?" She smirks as she makes her point.

"You are such a bitch sometimes," I inform her and her smirk turns into a full blown grin.

"Thanks," she says. "Now stop stalling."

"Well, if you must know, my lack of sleep has nothing to do with Blake."

"Oh, really?" she asks and I nod. "Mm hmm," she says obviously not believing me. Before I can react she grabs my scarf and pulls it off revealing my neck which has red blotches. "Explain this then," she says poking one of the marks in triumph.

"I got it from Tyler," I lie.

"Nuh uh, honey, don't you lie to me." She grabs my chin turning my face so she can see the other side of my neck. "That looks more like Tyler's work," she says poking one of the marks again. "All sloppy and he left only two as usual."

I snatch the scarf from out of her hand rewrapping it around my neck. "Leave me alone," I whine but she ignores me as usual.

"Now this side," she points to the side that has the most hickeys, "Is obviously work of someone you've never been with before, and since Blake was at your house last night and you two have never hooked up before, I'm guessing he did it." She lays her chin in her hand looking at me expectantly. "Now am I right or am I right?"

"How do you know that Blake was at my house last night?" I ask since I don't recall telling her about anything that happened last night.

"I'm going to take that as a yes," she says smirking at me and leaning back in her seat just as Mrs. Garcia begins to give us our assignment, leaving no time for me to question her anymore.

"Practice today is going to be longer than usual," Coach informs us when we walk into the gym for P.E.

"Why?" I ask.

"No," Jasmine complains before Coach can answer me. "I have a date." She crosses her arms over her chest poking her lip out. "I've been trying to schedule them around practice, and now you go and ruin that."

That girl's mouth is going to get her in a hell of a lot of trouble one of these days.

"You made a commitment to this team the day you signed your tryout papers," Coach says to Jasmine, sternness in her voice. "It's going to be longer today since there's going to be a couple of changes in the drills and we have to make it to the championship this season."

Last year our team was really good and we kicked ass all up until the tournament. We were up against FlagenGale (a horrible name, must I say?). We had already played them and killed them. The score was like 60-20 when we got to the tournament though it was like we just stopped playing. Me and Jasmine didn't get much playing time last year, seeing as we were sophomores, and Juniors and Seniors get the most time. Anyway, we got to the tournament and got our butts whooped. We didn't even make it to the championship.

"Don't worry, Coach, we got it this year," I say with a wave of my hand.

"We better," she warns, "And you two are excused from soccer practice today." With that she walks off and starts to give instructions to the other girls.

Jasmine and I both made soccer and basketball just like last year and the year before. Unfourtanetly, we can't fit both sports into our schedule fully. We usually get an hour of basketball and an hour of soccer. It sucks, but it's a good thing our games are never on the same day.

"Girls, go get dressed," Coach calls out and we start moving towards the locker room. Out of the corner of my eye I see Blake looking at me from the boys' side of the gym.

I change into my PE uniform and put my hair into a low ponytail.

"You may want to leave your scarf on," someone whispers into my ear and I think it's Jasmine until I turn around and come face to face with Mercedes Hall.

Mercedes is a bitchy senior who hates Jasmine and me. She's a basketball player too and we're better than her, but being older than us she gets more playing time. I used to think she hated us because we're better than her in basketball until I found out Jasmine hooked up with her boyfriend. Honestly Jasmine didn't know it was her boyfriend and he came onto her (I was there), so I don't see why she won't get over it.

"I see you're turning into a whore just like your friend," she says flipping her blond hair, "And to think I liked you a little." She scoffs.

"Who are you calling a whore?" Jasmine asks walking up beside me with her arms crossed over her chest as she glares at Mercedes. Mercedes is much taller than Jasmine but they're having a stare off like they're both giants.

"Girls, hurry up!" Coach calls out from her office that's connected to the locker room. She blows her whistle to make sure we got the warning.

Jasmine and Mercedes finally stop staring at each other and Mercedes flips her hair turning to leave.

"That's what I thought, bitch!" Jasmine says loud enough for Mercedes to hear. She simply flips her off. "I don't do girls!" Jasmine informs her as we walk out of the locker room and I shake my head.

I still have my scarf on with my uniform as I sit in the bleachers with Jasmine who's texting away furiously on her phone that she's not suppose to have out.

Coach walks out of her office and Jasmine sticks her phone in her bra. "You are so gross," I tell her shaking my head.

"Two compliments in one day, you're on a roll," she says smirking and I shake my head.

"Allison, why do you have that scarf on girl?" Coach calls out.

"I'm freezing," I lie wrapping my arms around myself and shivering as if I'm really cold.

She shakes her head but leaves me alone. "Alright, girls, today we're going to play volleyball with the boys," she says pointing to the volleyball nets that are up.

There's two up side by side on the opposite side of the half court line. "We're going to have two games going on - freshmen and sophomores on one side, Juniors and Seniors on the other." She holds up her roll sheet. "Don't cheat and go to whichever side you want; I'll know. Today I just want you to get comfortable but starting tomorrow I'll be judging your form while you serve and see if you actually try." She frees us to go to our appropriate nets and we do; the boys are already waiting so the game starts instantly.

We end up mixing the teams with girls and boys on both sides. I end up on the opposite team of Blake, Will, and Mercedes. I'm happy, though, that I have Jasmine and Daniel.

A kid from the other team serves the ball and it comes in my direction. Hell, no. I move out of the way as quick as I can and let someone else hit the ball. I do this the whole game; I guess I don't have to inform you that I suck at Volleyball.

The ball hits the ground and everyone frowns at me except for Blake and Jasmine, who simply look amused. "What?" I say frowning at them, "He was suppose to hit it," I say pointing at the tall boy next to me who looks just as lost as I am.

They know doggone well not to hit the ball to me. I flip my hair at them, moving away from the spot I was standing in.

"Nice save," Daniel says to me sarcastically with a bright smile.

I smile back at him, "Thanks," I say back just as sarcastically.

He chuckles before hitting the ball that came our way with a lot of force. I squeal running to stand behind Daniel and looking across the net to see Blake smirking.

That asshole.

When we're done playing I go back in the locker room, throwing on my basketball practice clothes instead of my regular ones.

"Are you seriously leaving that on?" Jasmine asks tugging at my scarf.

"Yea."

"I have no idea why you act like you're ashamed," she says shaking her head. "It only shows that boys want you."

"Allison!" Daniel calls walking over to me catching the attention of everyone in the room. Oh, goodness. He jogs over to me and some people stop staring but others continue to look.

"Look, another one of your admirers," Jasmine whispers in my ear before pulling my scarf off and jogging away from me to where Blake and Will are.

That bitch.

I panic as Daniel gets closer, he's definitely going to think I'm a whore.

I quickly throw my ponytail over my neck to the side with the most marks and put my hand on the side with the least.

"Hey Daniel," I say smiling at him and he smiles back.

"Something wrong with your neck?" he asks.

"Yea, I slept wrong," I lie, "And now it's sore." I almost shrug my shoulders but I realize that won't help my case.

"So..." he says rubbing the back of his neck nervously as I glare at Jasmine over his shoulder as she smirks at me. "I was wondering if you would want to go out..."

I snap my head back in his direction. "On a date, with me," he finishes shyly looking at me hopefully.

I give him a flirty smile. "Sure," I say.

His face brightens u., "Great," he says, "Uh, do you have a pen so I can write down your number?"

"Yea," I say reaching to get a pen out of my backpack.

"What's that on your neck Alli?" Mercedes says as if she's concerned about me as she walks by me and Daniel.

Daniel's eyes snap in the direction of my now uncovered neck.

Shit.

I turn my neck trying to hide it, but it's too late, he saw it. His eyes widen for a second but he doesn't say anything. I quickly grab his arm writing down my name and number. "Uh, well, bye," I say quickly before grabbing my backpack and storming over to Jasmine.

She tries to hide behind Blake but even if I didn't see her I would've heard her laughing a mile away. "Jasmine, I'm going to kill you."

"You'll have to get through Blake first." she says sticking her head out from behind him waving my scarf around.

I try to attack her but Blake grabs me and she runs behind Will using him as her shield now.

"Don't worry sweet cheeks," Blake whispers in my ear. "My mark looks good on you."

Chapter 8

"Allis," My mom calls out when I walk into the door of our home.

I let out a sigh closing the door behind me, "Yea mom?" I walk into the kitchen to find her dressed in one of her skimpy outfits drinking a glass of lemonade. Oh goodness, please don't say she's going out again.

"I'm going to need for you to do something for me." She informs me.

"What exactly?" I ask skeptically sitting on one of the bar stools.

"Well," She says leaning against the counter sitting her empty glass down. She eyes me, "You have to babysit for a friend of mine." She finally decides to tell me.

"What?" I ask as my jaw drops.

"Don't what me," she snaps glaring at me.

"Mom," I whine, "Children don't like me," I complain crossing my arms over my chest as if I'm five years old.

"Allison do you have a job?" My mom asks tapping her finger on the bottom of her chin.

"Uh no.."

Why is she asking me this, she knows the answer already.

"Mmm hmmm," she mutters, "And why is that?"

"Uh, because I have sports," I say a bit unsure. It feels like she's setting me up for something.

"Yes, so you have no job because of sports, not much responsibility," She concludes, "So you're going to babysit and that's final. This may teach you more responsibility seeing as you can't even take care of your car."

"But mom..." I start to whine but the glare she sends me instantly makes me shut up.

"Now come on, I'll drive you to the house, if you would've been home earlier we would've already been gone." She says grabbing her keys off the counter.

I'm assuming the house is where the demons I have to watch live. "Mom I had practice, it's not my fault." I try to justify as I follow her to the front door.

"Whatever, walk faster," She says opening the door while I try to catch up with her. This woman can walk fast for a fourth year old in heels.

I open the passenger door to my mom's red dodge dart. I've barely put my seatbelt on when mom starts to speed off, "Mom!"

"Oh sorry," she says barely sparing me a glance, "Look I'll get your car fixed in a month if you babysit whenever needed and don't give me back talk." She tells me when we come to a stop at a fairly big white house.

I start to weigh my options: Babysit demons for a month and get Antoinette back or Deal with Blake for longer than a month.

I let out a sigh, "Little demons here I come," I mutter.

My mother glares at me again, "Children aren't demons, their precious little angels, well except for you." She says as we get out of the car and start walking to the front door of the house.

The outside of the house is decent, there are roses and daisies in the garden that surrounds the whole front of the house. The pavement leading up to the house is black and gray looking bricks that stand out by the white house.

My mom rings the doorbell waiting patiently for the owner to come in. The door opens and before us stands a beautiful middle aged woman. She has nice green eyes that I've seen on someone before, her skin is fairly tan making it obvious she stays out in the sun, she's about the height of my mother and she has a very contagious smile. She has to be in her thirties at most.

"Hey Lydia," She says pulling my mom in for a short embrace before pulling away to look at me, "You must be Allison, you're mom has told me so much about you." She steps back out of the doorway, "Come in, I was almost ready." The last part was directed at my mom and I finally notice the woman's outfit.

She has on a knee length red dress that I'm sure she got from the Same place my mom has been getting her stuff lately. She has on red stilettos and a white purse to match the dress.

"I'm Rachel by the way," She informs me leading us to a room to wait for her.

I barely pay her any attention the only thing going through my head is 'this is a set up'. Rachel needs a babysitter so she can go out with my mom, (and more than likely Beatrice too). So of course since my mom is so generous (sarcasm) she decided to volunteer me without even asking. To top it off she's bribing me with Antoinette. This is not the freaking Hunger Games and I didn't volunteer as freaking tribute. I'm also pretty sure my name wasn't pulled from some stupid clear ball by That Effie chick.

"How many kids do you have?" I ask breaking out of my thoughts.

Please be one.

Please be one.

Wait, she wouldn't need this big house if there was only one child.

Dammit.

Please only have one child and just like living in big houses because you have the money.

Rachel looks at me hesitantly. Shit, that can't be good, "Umm.." She looks at the ground and back at me, "Three."

Three?

Holy Crap!

Three demons!

They expect me to deal with three of those suckers.

"How old are they?" I ask forcing a smile onto my face.

Rachel lets it a breath probably happy that I haven't run away, yet. "The twins are five, and the oldest is seven." She informs me, "I'll be right back I have to throw on some makeup and then I'll bring the kids down from their rooms." She says before scurrying up the stairs.

I turn to my mom ready to complain about Rachel having so many children but my mom silences me by holding up one finger.

"Don't start," She lets out a sigh frustration clear on her face, "Not today, just don't."

She's not yelling at me or angry but I know that something's bothering her, so for once I don't argue.

"Alright," I say leaning back on the couch, "Is Beatrice going out with y'all?" I ask trying to lighten the mood.

"Of course."

Footsteps on he stairs make me turn my head to see Rachel along with three children walking down the steps.

Rachel make the kids sit opposite of us on the other couch. "Kids, this is Allison, Allison, these are my kids." She says brightly, "This is Macey, Lacey, and Casey." She informs me gesturing to each kid as she says their names. Oh, so she's one of those parents who gives her kids similar names. Cute.

Macey has big green eyes,slightly tan but pale skin, curly brown hair, slight freckles on her nose that's barely noticeable but still cute. Lacey looks just like Macey except she has no freckles. I'm guessing they're the five year old twins. Casey (who's pouting by the way) is a cute,little seven year old with brown hair but its darker than the twins closer to black than brown, his eyes are also green, and his skin is tanner than the twins. I'm pretty sure I've seen an older version of him somewhere.

Lacey smiles at me revealing a mouth full of missing teeth,she's so cute. "I'm Lacey," she says brightly repeating what her mom already told me.

"I'm Allison," I say smiling back at her.

"Kids," Rachel says clearing her throat, "Tonight you're going to listen to your babysitters and do whatever they tell you to do, okay?" She informs them and the twins nod while Casey still sits with his arms folded across his chest.

I hear the front door open "You aunt Rachel I'm here" a familiar voice calls out and it starts to get closer, "Moms outside waiting for you."

Oh no.

Please don't be him.

Well it would explain the fact that Rachel and her kids resemble someone to me.

The one person who I really don't want to see turns the corner and as soon as he sees me a smirk appears on his face. "Well, well well, what are you doing here Sweetcheeks?"

"Blake, Allison's going to help you babysit tonight," Rachel says, "Your moms already told me you know each other, so I won't bother with introductions." She bends to give each of her children a kiss on the cheek. Casey wipes his off immediately.

"Gross Rachel!" He exclaims in a tiny boyish voice. Did he seriously just call her Rachel?

Demon.

"Don't call me that," Rachel says as her cheeks turn slightly red showing that she's either embarrassed or mad. I think it's the ladder.

She stands up straightly and I see hurt in her eyes. She turns heading for the door, "Call if you need anything."

"Be nice Allison," My mom warns me before her and Rachel leave slamming the door behind them.

There's silence in the room for a second before Casey walks over to Blake frowning at him. He stops in front of him crossing his arms over his chest, "Where have you been punk?"

Punk?

This child has to be the rudest thing ever.

"I've been busy," Blake says rubbing the back of his neck.

Does this kid seriously make him nervous?

Impossible.

"Your full of excuses." He complains before turning to glance at me, "Why did mom order the hooker to babysit us?"

My mouth drops open at his statement, what did I do to this child?

I don't even look like a hooker.

I glance down at my outfit. I look pretty normal in my practice clothes. Okay maybe they may look tight from being drenched in sweat, but a hooker? Come on.

"I don't know," Blake says with a shrug not denying the hooker part.

I scowl at him but he simply smirks.

"How about we go get out Call Of Duty?" He asks looking at Casey who instantly brightens up.

"Sure, I'll go get it out of my room."Casey runs up the stairs almost knocking over one of the twins. Macey, I think...

"Can we play in your hair?" One of them asks climbing on the couch next to me with big eyes and a pouty lip. She has no freckles, so it must be Lacey.

"Sure," I say not wanting to upset them because I can't deal with crying children.

Blake sits down on the couch beside me with two play station controllers in his hand. Macey squeezes in between us grabbing a portion of my hair roughly.

Ouch.

"You have pretty hair," Lacey says swinging the left side of my hair around in her little hands.

"Thank you," I say frowning when Macey pulls my hair again.

Casey comes pounding down the stairs with a video game in his hand. "I got it," he tells Blake who informs him to put it in the game console.

"Hey y'all are taking up the whole couch." Casey whines shoving Macey to make room for him to sit.

Did I mention Macey has a handful of my hair in her hand. Yea, that didn't turn out pretty.

I end up sitting on the floor while Macey and Lacey play in my hair and the boys play the game.

I'm actually shocked that Blake isn't bothering me, he's just being casual and nice playing games with Casey.

"I'm hungry," Casey whines after about thirty minutes.

I ignore him continuing to play temple run on my phone.

"Hey woman, go fix me some food," Casey says shoving my shoulder making me miss a jump on the game and I end up losing.

The little b-

Wait, he did not just tell me to go fix him some food.

I look over my shoulder to see Casey glaring at me and Blake trying to contain his laughter, "Food," Casey says clapping his hands at me, "Go make me some."

This time Blake doesn't contain his laughter he bursts out laughing while Casey has a serious look on his face.

Is he serious?

He really expects me to go make him some food.

"No." I say crossing my arms returning his glare.

"Your a woman, meaning you belong in the kitchen."

Sexist much?

This kid can't possibly be seven. What kind of stuff does he watch on TV?

"Blake." I whine turning to him for help but he shrugs.

"The kid has a point." He smirks at me.

I stand up making Macey and Lacey let go of my hair, I throw on cartoons before grabbing Blake's arm and pulling him to the kitchen with me. Its obvious he's letting me because he could easily stop me from pulling him.

"That child has serious issues." I mutter looking through the cabinets of the kitchen.

What in the hell am I suppose to make these children?

I can't even make myself food.

"Where are the noodles," I ask Blake who starts to laugh, "What?" I frown at him.

"Noodles really?" I nod my head and he simply smirks opening the fridge, "So your one of those girls who don't know how to cook. Well at least your pretty someone will marry you, maybe."

What did Blake just compliment and insult me at the same time. Well the insult isn't a surprise I'm already use to those, but he just called me pretty. Not hot, but pretty, looks like his nice side is out today.

"Reece." I say out loud.

"What?" Blake asks turning to me with a frown.

"That's going to be your new name for whenever you're being nice." I conclude sitting in a chair watching as he put some things onto the table.

"Your going to call me Reece?" He raises an eyebrow at me leaning against one of the counters with his arms tossed over his chest. I can see his muscles flex through his shirt and can't stop staring.

"Uh," I say finally looking up at his face to see that stupid smirk, dammit, he so saw me checking him out, "Yea," I finally manage to get out, "You call me Sweetcheeks all the time." I state.

"Well do you prefer babe 165?" He asks getting a cutting board out of the cabinet.

I glare at him "You are such an ass."

"Thanks." He grabs a knife out of the knife block, "Now come here," He beckons me towards him with the knife waving it in the air.

"Uh no," I say eying the knife.

Blake looks at the knife and then back at me a slow smile appearing on his face, "I know we don't get along much Sweetcheeks, which I'm starting to think is because of the sexual tension, but I don't plan on killing you." He reassures me making me scowl, "All the people I've killed never kissed me." He adds.

I kissed him?

I totally did not kiss him.

He kissed me.

"Uh," I stand up pointing a finger at him, "You kissed me," I exclaim glaring hard at him.

"The first time," He says holding up one finger "and it was a peck, then," He points his finger at me harshly, "You went and kissed me full on.' He accuses.

Okay, we'll maybe I did kiss him.

"But you kissed me first," I argue.

"Doesn't matter," He says twirling the knife around like it isn't lethal, "You still kissed me."

The kitchen door swings open and Macey walks in the room, she tugs on Blake's pants leg, "I'm hungry Blakey," She says looking up at him.

Blakey?

How cute.

Blake puts the knife down on the counter walking over to Macey, "Okay Mace, I'm making you something." He says patting her head gently, "And Allison's going to help." He says glancing over at me.

Like hell I'm going to help.

"Okay," She says before skipping out of the room.

"I am not going to help you." I tell him sitting back down in a seat at the table.

"Yea you are," He says walking over to me, he grabs one of my arms yanking me up roughly.

"Ow," I complain removing his hind off of me, "I don't cook."

He glances down at me with a bright smile on his face. "Well your gonna learn, my women have to know how to cook." He informs me patting the top of my head.

"I'm not one of your women," I say hitting his arm playfully not able to keep the smile off of my face.

"Oh look I made you smile," He brags leading me over to the cutting board.

"Whatever." I mutter looking at the board in disgust, "I hope you know I can't actually cut anything." I inform him.

"Great," He says with a bright smile on his face, "Stand here," He instructs pointing to the spot in front of the cutting board. He walks over to the fridge grabbing some stuff out.

"You can't boss me around," I mutter walking to the spot he told me to stand.

"I see you did what I told you to do." He says walking back over to me before leaning closer to me but he doesn't move in to do anything else.

I don't reply to him I simply stand still and wait for him to do something. He's close to me but not close enough to touch, if either of us move I'm pretty sure we'll be touching though. I can smell his cologne, I'm not sure what it is but it smells good. Minty, but there's a hint of something fruity, as contradicting as they are, they smell good.

Blake moves from behind me and I wonder what he's doing until he sets a bell pepper in front of me, "Here," He grabs my hand catching me off guard as he places a knife in my hand, "Im going to show you how to cut this." He says softly breath brushing by my ear.

I shiver a little but I don't say anything. Blake places his hand over mind catching me by surprise making me jump, "Relax," He says and I can practically see that smirk on his face. He raises our hands bringing the knife down on the bell pepper, I'm not sure if its intentionally or not but he moves closer making my back hit his front. The pepper splits in half and with his free hand he turns them over. He then proceeds to cut one vertically about ten times. He moves our hands above it and chop it horizontally into small pieces.

"Okay," He says releasing my hand but not moving away from me, "Try to do it yourself on the other half." he instructs me.

"Uh, okay," I study the other half for a second before bringing the knife down to cut it but Blake stops me.

"No, that's wrong, you don't bring the tip down, bring this part down," He rubs the blade of the knife not even worrying about being cut.

"And how exactly did you become an expert at cooking?" I ask bringing the knife down on the pepper the 'correct' way.

"Well Sweetcheeks that's a story for another time." He says moving away from me to get something else out of the cabinet.

I let out a sigh cutting the pepper how he did the other one. I let out a loud squeal causing Blake to drop a bowl out of his hand. "Shit girl, what's your problem?" He asks turning around to look at me with wide eyes.

"Look! Look!" I exclaim pointing at the pepper.

"It's cut," Blake states bluntly frowning at me picking up the bowl.

"But I did it," I state happily, "I the girl who burns water."

Blake walks over to me looking down at the pepper, the corners of his lips twitch a little, "You totally butchered this," He says picking up a big clunk of pepper, "Macey and Lacey will choke on this it's to big." He says and his lips turn up completely into a full blown smile, "Well not in that way but you get the punt."

I can't help but smile too even if he just insulted my cooking. "Oh shut up," I say shoving his arm and he smiles at me.

"Maybe next time Bambie," He says taking the nice from me to recut the peppers.

"Bambie?" I cross my arms turning my smile into a frown.

"Yea Bambie," He says smirking at me, gosh I hate that smirk, He looks down at my legs, "You have funny legs like a deer."

I look down at my legs turning them from side to side to look at them, "My legs are not funny." I shriek.

"Yes they are," He says kicking my right leg with the tip of his foot.

"Shut up," I say crossing my arms and sticking out my lip, "I play sports." I tell him.

"That's not an excuse," He says smiling, "They look so unhealthy, like crackhead legs, too skinny." he states taking seasoning out of the cabinet, "I think I can work with skinny legs." He says eying me, "As long as your good in bed."

My mouth drops open.

He did not just say that.

"You don't care what you say, do you?" I cross my arms over my chest.

"Nah," He says with a wave of his hand, "Throw some water on the stove would you, and don't burn it." He winks at me while I simply stare at him.

"Alli this taste good." Lacey says smiling at me as she eats her pasta.

"She didn't make it," Blake says with a scowl on his face.

"Hey," I protest, "I boiled the water and cut a pepper."

"That definatelty makes you a professional Bambie." He says sarcastically shoving a spoon full of food into his mouth. Yes a spoon.

Who in the heck eats pasta with a spoon?

I asked Blake that.

His reply?

Forks are for wimps and a something else that I won't repeat, I'll give you a hint: It's a part only us girls have.

"Shut up," I mutter popping some pasta and chicken in my mouth.

He starts to laugh gathering the kids dirty plates and putting them in the dishwasher. "Are y'all ready for your baths?" He asks the kids and they all nod except for The Stubborn Casey.

"Go on up Casey," Blake instructs not giving him an option, "Sweetcheeks take Lacey and Macey up." He tells me as if I work for him.

"Please is a nice word," I say sarcastically grabbing both Lacey and Macey's hands leading them upstairs. "Which one is the bathroom?" I ask them looking around.

Macey points at a door decorated in pink crowns."That ours."

"Okay." I say walking them to the bathroom throwing open the door.

I'm consumed in nothing but pink and purple when I walk through the door. The walls are fully pink with the Disney princesses on the walls along with purple polka dots. The shower curtain has Cinderella on it and the seat cover has Tatiana.

Lacey and Macey get towels out of the cabinet and I realize I have no idea what I'm suppose to do.

"Blake?" I call out sticking my head out of the door.

Blake comes running up the stairs, "What happened?" He asks looking concerned.

"Nothing," I say and he frowns, "What am I suppose to do?" I ask gesturing to the bathroom where the twins are.

"That's what you called me up here for," He shakes his head, "Just make sure they don't slip in the tub or anything, and that they fully clean themselves." He says shaking his head again, "You're such an idiot Bambi." He flicks my nose before quickly making his way downstairs.

Asshole.

I walk back into the bathroom closing the door behind me. Macey and Lacey start to strip out of their clothes as I start to run the bath water. After they're done I wrap them in their towels and they lead me to their room to get their clothes.

Man, if I though after seeing the bathroom I wouldn't see anything else with a lot of pink man I was wrong. Their room's walls are pink as well but instead of princesses everything is covered in Minnie Mouse.

This is just sad.

I open the girls dressers getting out their matching pajamas and under-wear. I wait on the bed with my back turned as they change. I know it's weird since I saw the, shower, but I don't want to just sit here and stare as they change. That's kind of stalkerish.

"We're done Alli," Macey says grabbing one of my hands. Lacey grabs my other hand and we walk down the stairs to find Blake and Casey watching wrestling.

"Hey," I protest sitting down on the couch next to Blake, "We don't want to watch wrestling." I complain snatching the remote from out of Blake's hand.

"We were here first," Blake argues trying to snatch the remote from me.

"Nu uh," I say wagging my finger in front of his face, "Now Blakey, be considerate and let's watch something we all enjoy." I tell him flipping through the stations.

"Sponge Bob!" All the kids shriek at the same time. Well at least that's what I made out, I'm pretty sure the twins said "Swonge Wog."

Oh no.

No.

No.

No.

I hate this stupid show with that gay sponge and star.

The kids start bouncing up and down with joy. Looks like I have to watch this show.

"I'm squished," Casey complains shoving Blake closer to me, close enough that we're touching.

Macey climbs in my lap before laying across me and Blake. I scoot over closer to Lacey since there's more room now.

"No." Macey whine, "My head fall now." She says gesturing to the gap now in between me and Blake.

I sigh scooting back over to Blake and I see him smirk from the corner of my eye. About five minutes into the show Macey is already snoring. I feel Blake shift next to me before his arm stop touching mines and ends up on the back of the couch behind me. A couple of minutes after that Lacey's now sleep and her head is resting on the portion of my lap that Macey isn't taking up. I feel something drop onto my shoulders and realize its Blake's arm.

I don't complain, I find myself getting more comfortable, relaxing against him. Blake stiffens for a a second before relaxing again, his hand cups my shoulder pulling me closer to him.

I'm not doing this.

I'm not going to get comfortable with Blake.

The Blake who finds it funny to bother me twenty four seven.

Well it's not like anythings going to happen, and we've barely argued all day.

Oh screw it.

I lean my head on Blake's shoulder and stare at the TV.

When does this crap ever go off?

"Can we watch something else since the girls are sleep?" Casey asks Blake.

Maybe he isn't too bad.

Case frowns at us, "Ill, you two are gross, girls have cooties," He says, "Blake your gonna be sick."

Cooties?

Blake chuckles rubbing the side of my arm where Casey can't see, "Girls don't have cooties Casey, they have something worst STDS." Blake explains to him, "Oh, and they're definitely not gross, you'll grow to love what they can give, but that's a lesson that'll have to wait for a while."

Oh, he did not say that.

"Look basketball's on," Blake says changing the subject.

"Yes," Casey cheers "It's The Celtics, they're going to kick the heats ass."

He cusses? And what does Blake do? Nothing. My goodness.

"Like heck they are," I say "The Heat is much better." I declare looking at the TV.

"It's okay Allison," Case says reaching over to pay my knee with his small hand, "The children are sleep, you can swear.

I stare at him mouth hanging open while Blake simply laughs.

It takes a good two hours and two basketball games for Casey to go to sleep.

"I'm going to take them upstairs," Blake whispers in my ear as I'm nodding off.

"Okay," I mutter moving my head off of his shoulder watching as he wraps his arm Mace taking her out of our laps. He kicks the bottom of Casey's leg, "Hey man, wake up." He says when Casey's eyes open a little bit.

Casey mutters something and lazily gets off the couch leaning against Blake. Blake shifts Macey so that she's laying over his left shoulder. He picks up Lacey putting her on his right shoulder. With Blake still basically leaning on him he takes them all to their rooms.

I lay down on the whole couch closing my eyes listening to the sounds of the people cheering at the basketball game on the TV. I hear footsteps on the couch before the TV is shut off. I open my eyes when my head is lifted up for a second before being laid on something else. I look up into Blake's eyes before re closing mine.

"Do you know how bad your hair is?" Blake asks and I feel his fingers moving through my hair, "You shouldn't let the twins experiment again."

I chuckle softly opening my eyes to look at him, "Do you know how un badass you are?" I state.

Everyone always go on and on about how bad Blake's suppose to be but, but I haven't seen him do a thing that's bad at all.

Well, he did say earlier that he killed someone.

Come to think about it...

"Did you really kill someone?" I ask searching his green eyes.

His eyes dark for a second before going back to normal, "Another story for another day." He says repeating what he said earlier.

Oh my goodness.

Blake totally killed someone, there wouldn't be another discussion for another day if he didn't kill someone.

Okay, calm down Allison, if Blake wanted to kill you he would have already.

Plus he said he doesn't kill people who kiss him.

"Well story can I hear for today?" I ask trying to calm my nerves.

"Relax Allison I'm not an axe murderer," He says softly rubbing my arm, "Well, you can hear about when I lost my virginity, if you want." He says with a smirk.

"Your so gross," I say reaching up to pinch his nose, "Im being serious."

"Me too," He says smiling removing my hand from his nose, "Well lets see, I got into my first fist fight in pre school because this kid wouldn't give me his jello, and I like jello." He says rubbing the bottom of his chin.

"I want to know something serious," I whine sticking my lip out.

"Okay, okay, I can't say no when you do that," He says taking a deep breath growing serious, "When I was nine," he says not looking at me anymore but looking forward as he plays with my hair, "I came home to find my mom crying, I had no idea why. Being a young boy I had no idea what to do so I sat there and watched her cry. Then," his jaw clenches a little, "I noticed my dad was nowhere to be found, long story short my dad, h-he was a gang member, owed some people some money, didn't pay it, got killed. Well to be more specific he was decapitated." He concludes.

Wow.

He just told me this story like it was just normal. He made it short and clipped.

Well, I asked for something serious, I just wasn't expecting that.

"So there you have it, something serious to know about me." He says with a tight smile, "Oh and I'm on parole until its over I can't get into any trouble." A real smile makes its way onto his face now even though it still seems forced, "So never question my bad assness, I'm definitely bad ass."

I chuckle, "You are so conceited," I mutter closing my eyes and yawning.

"And you are too innocent I'm going to change that." He informs me running his finger along my cheek.

We continue to stay how we are and eventually I fall asleep with Blake stroking my hair.

"Allison," a voice says as I'm being shaken, "Wake up, we have to get home." The persons words are slurred and I know it's my mother.

I can't smell anything but alcohol. With a groan I open my eyes looking at my mother, "Alright I'm coming."

I hear her walk away and something shifts from underneath me. I look up to see Blake opening his eyes rubbing the back of his neck.

I sit up stretching, "Maybe you shouldn't sleep like that next time, I doubt you'd have to deal with a crook in your neck then." I inform him.

"It's your fault," he mutters standing up.

"Whatever," I say smiling a little making my way towards the door.

Well maybe babysitting won't be so bad.

"Hey Allison!" He calls out from behind me and I turn to see him smiling, "Did I mention earlier to stop kissing me?"

Just maybe.

Chapter 9

"Hey can we work on the project at your house, again?" Jasmine asks me as soon as I get to school.

"Why not?" I say rubbing my eyes. After leaving Rachel's house last night I couldn't go back to sleep. Now I have bags under my eyes, again, thanks to Blake. Yes, I'm blaming Blake, if he wouldn't have let me go to sleep in the first place at Rachel's house, I would've been able to sleep when I got home. I mentioned it to him this morning when he came to pick me up for school, and you know what? He said I should have taken sleeping peels.

"You look tired," She states poking me in the shoulder as we walk to home room.

"Just a little," I tell her opening the door to our classroom and letting her walk in in front of me. The only people in the class is Blake, Will, and the girls they're flirting with.

You've got be kidding me.

I wouldn't be so pissed if they weren't crowding my desk. "Out of the way," Jasmine says pushing one of the petty blondes off of her desk. The girl almost lands on the floor but Will catches her, sending a glare to Jasmine, "What?" She throws her hands up, "She was on my desk." She points at the girl who backs away from her. The girl's friend hops off of my desk, I guess in fear of Jasmine.

I take my seat next to Jasmine who's avoiding Will's glare, "That's the power of being the only black girl in this class," She whispers to me and I let out a chuckle.

Jasmine always makes jokes about her being black so people are scared of her because they think she's the "crazy black ghetto girl." The first time she told me I laughed but then I noticed that people really do see her as that. Well, I have no problem with it because it makes them leave me alone in fear that Jasmine will kick their butts.

"Hey, stop glaring at me before I slap it off your face." Jasmine threatens Will in a harsh voice.

Will stops glaring at her and instead turns his back to us as he talks to Blake. Come to think of it, Blake hasn't bothered me yet. Hmmm, that's kind of weird. I glance over to see that he's just casually talking to Will. There's nothing off about him, he looks the same that he did thirty minutes ago when we got here.

The teacher walks in the classroom and Blake and Will take their seats. "Today, your going to work with your group for the project, this is the only class time I'm going to give you." She states before going to her desk and working on her computer.

"No, you can shoot the video, so no one will have to see your distorted face." Jasmine tells Will as she crosses her arms over her chest.

"No, you should shoot the video, because your boobs would take up the whole screen." Will argue backs as he stands over Jasmine who's sitting on my couch, "What do you wear, a triple Z?"

My mouth drops open but Jasmine doesn't seem to be offended, "Are you mad that I have book boobs, but you have a small d..."

That's where I stop listening to the conversation. Once again we are all at my house working on the project, and Jasmine and Will are arguing, again. We got some work done at school but not much. We were almost sent out of the classroom because of Jasmine and Will's loud arguing so we decided to quit working until we got to my house, where they can be as loud as they want.

I don't think that was a good idea.

"Jasmine put the vase down." I hear Blake say as he stands up walking towards Jasmine but it's too late, she's already thrown it at Will. Luckily, Will had the common sense to duck which makes the vase fly over his head.

"Oh my god!" I say loudly slapping Jasmine's hand as she reaches for something else to throw, "What is y'all's problem."

They both remain silent as they glare at each other.

"I know what it is," Blake interjects, "It's the sexual tension." He states cleverly as he rubs his chin.

"Like hell it is!" Jasmine exclaims.

At the same time Will says, "Sexual tension my ass."

"It's okay, you don't have to lie." Blake says just as my phone starts to ring. Jasmine and Will continuously argue with him as I leave the room to answer my phone.

"Hello," I say into the iPhone after I make it to the kitchen.

"Hello," A deep voice says, "Is this Allison?"

I scrunch my eyebrows together, "Yea, Who is this?" I ask as I lean against the wall.

"Daniel." The voice answers just as the kitchen door opens.

"Oh hey Daniel," I say just as I look up and meet the eyes of Blake.

Aw, hell.

"So I was wondering.." Daniel says going off into a sentence but I can't hear him because I'm too focused on Blake who's walking towards me.

Crap.

"Allison?" Daniel asks in an unsure voice as I try to walk away from Blake.

"Yea, I'm here, what were you saying?" I ask still watching Blake who smirks at me.

"Our date, what do you think of going to the fair?"

I end up with my back against another wall with Blake standing in front of me with his devilish smirk on his face. "Stay away." I mouth to him but its to late he's already put his hands on either side of my head and is leaning in close to me.

"Uh, yea, the fair sounds nice." I say "nice" coming out kind of strangled since Blake shocked me when he kissed my neck. I try shoving him away with one hand but I give up.

"Are you okay?" Daniel asks with genuine concern in his voice.

"Yes," I say and if comes out as a squeak. Blake pulls back for a second to smirk at me before grabbing my phone out of my hand and snapping it close.

My eyes widen in shock, "You did not just..." The rest of my sentence is cut off as he puts a finger to my lip to shush me.

My phone rings again and Blake ends up turning it off before going back to kissing my neck.

We are not doing this, not again.

"Jasmine and Will..." I manage to get out worried about them walking in the room on us. I could easily say that Blake attacked me, which wouldn't be a complete lie.

"They're gone." He says in my ear sending a shiver down my spine. Just as he starts to work on my neck again we hear the front door open.

Oh goodness.

I push Blake away from me just as my mom and Beatrice walk in the kitchen laughing loudly.

"Hey kids," My mom says sitting bags down on the kitchen table.

Blake sends me an all too familiar glare and I turn away from him to look at my mom. "Hey," I say casually, as I walk over to the fridge.

"Good news." Beatrice says and I look up from the fridge knowing "good news" means "bad news."

"What?" I ask closing the fridge door and sitting at the kitchen table with my back to Blake.

"Well, we're going out of town this weekend," My mom starts and that's all I need to know to figure out this is yet another set up, "And Rachel is coming with us."

"Who's watching the kids?" Blake asks suspiciously finally speaking.

"Well that's what we were getting to," Beatrice says taking a sip of her coke that she had when she walked into the kitchen, "You guys are going to watch them of course."

"Oh and what happened to my vase?" My mom asks as I stare at her in shock.

Chapter 10

"Hey Allison," Someone calls out from behind me as I'm headed out of school. I turn around to see Daniel running up to me with a smile on his face. I return the smile as I wait for him to catch up to me.

"Hi," I say when he finally catches up to me and we start walking to the parking lot. I glance down at my watch and let out a sigh, I have to be at Rachel's house by 5:30 to start watching the kids.

"So about our date tonight," Daniel says as we make it to Blake's car.

What does he mean date? Our date isn't tonight.

"What date?" I ask leaning against Blake's car.

"You remember I called you about it the other day," He says scratching the back of his neck.

Hmm, I don't remember that.

"You hung up on me..." He trails off looking at me expectantly.

Aw crap. I was too focused on Blake to really listen to Daniel. I'm going to kill that stupid jerk, he's always messing up my concentration. I have to freaking babysit tonight, I can't go out on a date.

"Well about that-"

"She can't, she has other plans." Well speak of the devil.

Blake wraps an arm around my shoulder smirking at Daniel, "We have to do something, so she can't come." He continues.

Daniel looks nervous as he looks at us, "I didn't know that you two are together." He says pointing at us awkwardly.

"We aren't together," I say pushing Blake's arm off of my should glaring at him.

"Uh, okay, so you can go on the date tonight, right?" He asks with a hopeful look on his face.

I shake my head at the same time that Blake says, "Nope." In a too cheerful voice.

Daniel's face falls and I start to feel really bad but I can't get out of babysitting. "Maybe we can just hang out at the house, because I have to babysit." I suggest.

Daniela's face brightens again and a smile that's cuter than puppies (almost) comes onto his face replacing the frown. "Sure, that'll be cool, just text me the address."

"Okay, bye." He walks away with that smile on his face as I push Blake out of my way to get into the car.

"Hey, watch it, you can't be pushing all on this sexy body." He says walking to the driver's side of the car and getting in the car.

I slam my door causing him to glare at me but I don't even care, "You're such an ass." I inform him.

"Why, thank you." He says smiling as he pulls out of the parking lot.

"Can't you just babysit the kids on your own while I go out on a date?""

"Nope." He says popping the 'p'.

I cross my arms over my chest leaning back into the seat.

He always has to go and ruin everything for me.

"Just make sure, you don't give the kids orange juice, they're highly allergic." Rachel informs me as she bends down to give the twins a kiss on their cheeks. I'm surprised that Casey actually lets her kiss him considering he's such an evil brat.

"Okay." I answer, "Have you talked to Blake?" I ask her since he was suppose to be here at the same time I was but he hasn't arrive or called. My mom drove me here, making sure I came on time, but hat asshole is MIA.

"No, I'm pretty sure he'll come though, so don't worry." She reassures me with a half smile before leaving with my mother and Blaire.

I turn to the twins and the demon who are just looking at me. "So.." I trail off nervously, "How about we watch movies." The words are barely out of my mouth before they all run off in different directions.

What the hell?

"Hey get back here!" I call out running in the direction I think I saw Macey go in.

I hear someone giggling from the girl's bedroom. "Hey you." I say as I spot Macey hiding under the bed, "Come here." I tug her from under the bed throwing her over my shoulder.

I could've swore that they were sweeter last time, I thought I would only have to worry about Casey, but I guess not.

"Lacey!" I call out, "I have Macey, aren't you going to come help out your twin?" I call out trying to persuade her to come out of her hiding spot.

I feel something hit me in the back of my legs and I turn around to see Lacey beating on me. I guess that's her plan to save Macey.

"Stop it." I say grabbing her and throwing her over my other shoulder. I'm happy that they seem to weigh less than 30 pounds.

"Casey!" I call out just as the doorbell rings. That better be Blake.

I stomp down the stairs with both twins still on my shoulder. I fling open the door trying not to drop one of the girls.

"Oh hey Daniel." I say pulling a smile on my face as Lacey starts to beat on my back again. "Stop that, dang it." I tell her almost tempted to drop her on her head.

This is why I don't like children.

"Hey." Daniel says as his eyes flicker to the children nervously.

"I'm sorry, you can come in." I say moving out of the doorway. He walks in closing the door behind him taking in the house.

"Nice." He says as I lead him into the living room.

"Thanks, but it's not mines." I confess, "You can just sit." I tell him putting the twins down on the love seat, "Stay," I warn them. I turn to Daniel plastering a smile on my face, "I'll be back."

I march up the stairs in frustration, "Casey, being your butt out here, I don't have time for this." I warn opening the bedroom doors but not spotting him. I open the bathroom door and am doused with water. It's cold and is in my hair and all over my clothes. You've got to be kidding me. "Casey!" I shriek as the demon tries to run past me but I grab him by his shirt, "I'm going to kill you." I say gritting my teeth.

"I'm going to tell Blake that you threatened me." He says as I drag him downstairs by his shirt sleeve.

"Well you won't be able to because I'm going to kill him too." I inform him throwing him on the love seat with the twins when we get into the living room.

"What happened?" Daniel asks with wise eyes taking in my now soaking body.

"Children, that's what happened." I say angrily looking at the kids. "Stay here, and watch cartoons if any of you move from this spot you'll be sleeping outside with the monsters tonight, okay?" The twins eyes widen in fear and I smirk, that'll teach them. Casey just glares at me with his arms across his chest.

I march up the stairs grabbing a towel out of the bathroom to wrap around my hair. I don't have anything to put on besides pajamas since I have to wear my other clothes tomorrow and Sunday, if I'm here, (I'm really thinking about abandoning these demons.)

Where in the hell is Blake?

This is all his stupid fault.

I let out an aggravated sigh walking back down the stairs with the towel still wrapped around my head.

"Why are you here?" I hear Casey asks as I'm making my way back down the stairs, "You know Allison doesn't like you, your a dic-" I rush down the stairs covering Casey's mouth before he can finish his sentence.

How in the hell does he even know that word?

Daniel looks uncomfortable as he shifts in his seat.

There's a wetness on my head and I pull it back. "Did you just lick me?" I ask Casey in shock.

"Yeap." He says with a smirk on his face.

"Time out, go get in the time out corner." I tell him pointing to the corner of the room.

"Timeout?" He looks up at me in shock, "I'm too old for timeout." He says remaining on the couch.

This child is getting on my last nerves.

The front door opens and I hear laughing as Will and Blake walk into the room with a bunch of bags. "Oh hey Allsion." Will says giving me a smile brighter than the stars.

"What happened to you?" Blake asks with amusement in his eyes as he takes in my appearance.

"You." I state glaring at him.

"Wow, I didn't know I was so good that I could get you wet without being in your presence." He winks at me and I let out an aggravated noise stomping out of the room and walking into the kitchen.

I'm going to kill Blake, along with his cousin (Casey), I still have a soft spot for the twins so they can live.

The kitchen door opens and Blake walks in with a satisfied look on his face.

"You were suppose to be here an hour ago." I say glaring at him with my arms crossed over my chest.

"I had to make a pit stop." He says not even fazed by my glare, "Oh, why did you threaten to kill Casey, he's not too happy about that." He says with a forced frown because there's still amusement in his face.

"Because he threw water all on me, after making me run after him upstairs." I tell him.

He simply laughs and I lunge at him.

I'm not sure what I was going to do, maybe tackle him, but he captures my wrist ruining my plan.

"Now Allsion," He says in a mocking tone backing me up until I'm against the wall, "That wasn't nice." He says holding my hands over my head.

"Get off of me." I say as I start to burn up and my heart beats faster. I can barely tell that I'm soaked in water since my full concentration is on Blake,

"Why would I do that?" He asks in amusement moving closer to me. Our faces are so close that one move and we'll kiss.

His breath fans my face smelling of mint.

That's all it takes for me to close the space between us mashing my lips to his.

Okay, have I mentioned that boys with minty breath is my weakness?

I feel Blake smile against my lips before he returns the kiss. The kiss isn't all sweet and one that makes the audience go "aww." No it's rough and possessive. He lets go of my hands and I wrap them around his neck as he brings his around my waist. My wet body presses against his dry one but I'm barely aware of it. Blake's tongue slides across my lip just as the door opens. "Hey Allison..." Daniel cuts off when he sees me and Blake together.

Dammit.

I push Blake away from me and he willingly backs away. I'm speechless as I look at Daniel, "Maybe I should just go." He says nervously backing out of the kitchen.

Crap.

I push past Blake following behind Blake, but it's too late Daniel's already out if the house.

How could I be so stupid? Going an kissing Blake while Daniel's in the other room. I don't even like Blake because he's a big asshole it's just the attraction. An attraction that just made a hot nice guy walk out on me. I let out a frustrated sigh stomping into the living room where Will is watching TV with the kids.

I walk into the kitchen looking for Blake but he's not even in here.

"Where's Blake?" I ask Will walking back into the living room.

"Upstairs in the guest room." He says pointing towards the staircase. I stomp up the stairs making my way to the guest room that Rachel showed me earlier.

I'm going to give that bastard a piece of my mind. Show him that he can't just try and seduce me anytime he wants.

When I fling the door open the first thing I see is a well toned shirtless back. The only thing out of place that I see is a scar in the lower right part of the back. Dammit, how am I suppose to holler at him about seducing me when he's shirtless.

Blake turns around and when he sees me gawking at his body he smirks. "See something you like?" He leans against the wall folding his arms over his chest.

"I thought there was a bug on you," I lie pitifully causing him to chuckle.

"Well thanks for looking out for me." He says sarcastically with that stupid but hot smirk still on his face.

"Just put on a shirt," I say looking down at the ground to avoid meeting his eyes, or just simply gawking at his body again.

"Why Allison?" He asks in a mocking tone and I can hear him taking steps towards me, "Does me being shirtless bother you?"

Being smarter this time I don't back up into a wall, nope instead I back out of the room. My back hits the wall outside of the door and I swear.

The one time I do something smart, and I still end up trapped.

That's just sad.

Blake puts his hands on either side of my head and buries his nose in the crook of my neck making me shiver. It doesn't help that I'm still kind of wet from Casey pouring water on me.

Suddenly Blake grabs me by my waist spinning me around so that he's now backing me up back into the room.

This can't be happening, I came in here to put an end to this, but it's just going to happen again.

Blake closes the door behind us, pushing me back onto the bed (not rough, but not gentle either.)

"Blake," I say in a warning tone as he hovers above me before kissing my neck.

"Hmm." Is all he says causing a small vibration on my neck.

"We can't do this," I say as he pushes me back fully on the bed.

"And why not?" There's a wetness on my neck now from his tongue flickering across my soft spot.

"Because we hate each other." I complain.

"Hate is a strong word," He tells me placing kisses along my neck and shoulder blade.

"Blake, stop it." I complain but it comes out weak and I know that I'm caving in.

Blake pulls back from my neck looking down at me with a smirk on his face, "You really don't want me to stop now do you?" He asks slightly brushing his lips against mine.

And there goes that mint breath again.

I wrap my arms around his neck pulling his face against mine. His lips are soft and plump against my dry ones. Blake licks my lips and I can't help but think that my dry lips problem is over. Just as I'm about to part my lips the doorbell rings downstairs.

Blake lets out an aggravated groan before rolling off of me.

I push myself off the bed standing up, "You have got to stop doing that." I say pointing an accusing finger at him.

"You kissed me first." He states.

"Well because you came at me shirtless." I say getting more frustrated by the second.

"Are you saying that you can't resist my shirtless body?" He smirks at me and my mouth drops open.

Instead of continuing to argue with him I simply leave the room and march down the steps. I hear Blake's laughter as he follows behind me.

I stop at the bottom of the stairs when I see the living room.

You have got to be kidding me.

The living room is full of teenagers hanging out and drinking.

How did I not here this all going on?

In the back corner of the room Will is trying to hook up a stereo system with some other dude.

I turn around to look at Blake knowing damn well he has something to do with this.

"Did I mention that we're having a party?" He asks with a smirk on his face.

Chapter 11

A party.

A freaking party.

Blake threw a party, without confronting me.

He's so dead.

"Blake!" I yell in rage and he cringes away from me even though there's still amusement in his face.

"What?" He asks leaning against the railing of the stairs.

"I'm going to kill you!"

"You just love threatening to kill people, huh?" He smirks at me and I want to punch him even more.

"The kids are here!" I yell at him.

"Correction, the kids are in the twin's room with Jasmine," He looks across the room at Will, "Will's going to help her watch them after he's done hooking up the stereo."

Just as Blake finishes his sentence the floors start to shake from the bass of the stereo, and music fills the room. People erupt in. Here's and I shake my head.

"Blake!" I scream at him once again.

He smirks, "Sorry, I can't hear you." With that he walks off bumping my shoulder.

That bastard knows he heard me because I could hear him. I let out a frustrated sigh as Will walks by me with an apologetic look on his face. I don't say anything I simply stomp down the rest of the stairs and walk into the living room. There are teenagers everywhere and alcohol is being passed around.

What was Blake thinking? Alcohol in the house with the kids. He's lost whatever piece of mind he still had left.

I bump into someone since I'm so confused in my thoughts. "Oh I'm sorry," I say as the person steadies me by grabbing my arms. I look up to see Ryan Freeman.

He looks down at me and smiles, "Hey Allison."

"Hi," I say not at all oblivious to the fact he's still holding onto my arms. It's not like his hold is tight or anything, just sort of uncomfortable since I barely know him.

"So, nice part, huh?" He finally release his hold on me and backs up one step since we were standing pretty close.

Nice party?

Yea, right.

"No, actually I didn't even know about it." I admit crossing my arms across my Chest feeling sort of self conscious.

Ryan makes a weird face, "Then why are you here?"

"Oh, I was babysitting the kids who stay here." I tell him shifting from foot to foot, nervously.

He raises an eyebrow indicating that he's still confused.

"Well, I was babysitting with Blake, but Blake decided to throw a party without letting me know." I explain hoping he finally understands what I'm saying.

"Oh, now it all makes sense," He gives me a small smile that makes me blush since its so cute.

Oh my god, I'm becoming such a whore. First I kiss Blake while I'm suppose to be on a sort of date with Daniel. Now after I made out with

Blake I'm thinking about how cute Ryan's dimples are. What in the hell is wrong with me?

I feel an arm drape down on my shoulder and someone's body heat on my side. "Hi, Ryan."

As soon as the person talks I know who it is.

"Hey Blake." Ryan says taking another step away from me as if he's nervous.

"I'm going to borrow Allison for a dance, so she'll talk to you later." I can hear the smirk in Blake's voice as he drags me away from Ryan.

"Your such an asshole." I say to him over the music when we get to the make shift dance floor in the living room. I cross my arms over my chest and glare at him while he smirks at me.

"What are you talking about?" He looks down at me trying to put on an innocent face, "I just want to dance with you."

"Liar," I mutter under my breath as Blake places his hands on my hips sending tingles through my body.

He leans down close to my ear, whispering, "I hope you know how to dance."

I don't know how long Blake and I have been dancing but sweat is now dropping from my body and people are watching us. Finally I lay my head on Blake's shoulder and let out a tired breath. I feel him shaking with laughter beneath me and I have no idea why, but a smile forms on my lips.

He wraps his arm around my waist dragging me off upstairs to the twin's room. The kids are bouncing around while Will and Jasmine are arguing about something.

"You guys are horrible babysitters." Blake says watching them in amusement.

They both jump and look at us indicating they hadn't even notice us walk in the room.

Jasmine stands up with a grateful look on her face, "Good, you're here to relieve us, I can't deal with him for another second." At first I think she's talking about Casey but she points at Will. She turns her nose up at him, making me and Blake laugh, before she starts walking out of the room.

"How do you think I feel?" Will exclaims following her out of the room.

"Alli!" Macey yells hugging my legs as Lacey reaches for me to pick her up.

"I'm sweaty, I can't pick you up Lace." I tell her giving her a small smile.

She sticks out her bottom lip in a pout as Blake closes the door to the room. Casey looks at Blake in relief, "Can we watch Basketball?"

"Sure." Blake tells him grabbing the remote off the twins nightstand.

Lacey rubs her eyes and looks back up at me, "Sleepy." She says grabbing her teddy bear off her bed.

"Okay well go to sleep then." I say helping her into bed before helping Macey into hers.

"Story." Lacey says passing me a book. I look at the cover seeing that the book is "Cinderella." Blake sits on the floor in front of Macey's bed with Casey watching the game.

"Okay," I sit down in between their beds opening the book, "Once upon a time."

"The end." I close the book looking up to see the twins fast asleep. Blake took Casey to his room a while ago when he fell asleep, and I told him to go back to the party.

I place the book back onto their bookshelf turning off their lamps. I make my way to the door closing it behind me when I leave. The party is still as loud as it was two hours ago and even more people have shown up. I walk into the kitchen grabbing a pack of sealed chips. I really want something to drink but I know enough about parties, that I know date rate drugs go around.

I find a familiar curly brown haired guy in the living room flirting with girls.

"Hey Allison." David says giving me a smile when he sees me forgetting about his groupies.

"Hey," I say with a sigh sitting on the couch next to him, "Where's Lexi?" I ask looking around for his girlfriend.

"Oh, we broke up." He informs me with a slight smile even though its kind of sad, "I'm back on the market." He doesn't sound too happy about it like he usually does when he breaks up with someone.

"Why so sad?" I ask raising a brow at him.

"I'm not," He mutters, and I know I'm not going to get an answer out of him, at least not today.

"Okay," I say standing up and ruffling his hair. He slaps at my hand and I laugh before looking for Jasmine.

I find her on the other side of the house in the more quiet part of the house. "Hey Boo, what's up?" I ask noticing that her face doesn't look to happy.

"Nothing." She says in a grouchy tone.

"Really?" I bump he shoulder with mines, "Because you sound pretty posed."

She looks at me and lets out a sigh, "No it's just that.." She trails off running a frustrated hand through her hair as her gaze lands across the room.

I follow he gaze seeing Will and Blake talking to a group of girls. My heart drops a bit for unknown reasons, but I ignore it. I look at Jasmine again seeing hurt in her eyes. "You like Will don't you?" I ask already knowing the answer. I've known Jasmine my whole life and I've only seen her really like someone once. She looked the same way she looks now.

"Of course not," She lies not looking me in the eyes.

"Then why are you looking at him like that?"

"Why did you kiss Blake when Daniel was here earlier?" She shoots back raising a brow at me.

I stay silent and so does she.

Chapter 12

"I don't know who's going to clean this up, but it's definitely not going to be me." I tell Blake glaring at him with m arms crossed across my chest.

It's the morning after Blake's stupid party and the house is totally trashed. There's red solo cups everywhere, crushed snacks, and not to mention a couple of people are still passed out on our floor. Blake himself is just as trashed as the house. His hair is flying everywhere in a not so cute way. His eyes are barely open and he's squinting, his hand is to his head holding it as he leans against the wall of the living room.

"Allison, why are you so loud?" He groans out pressing his hands to his ears, to drown me out I guess.

"I'm not loud, you just have a bad hangover, but you need to get over it and clean this shit up." I frown a him gesturing to the messy room.

"No, I'll get someone else to do it, just let me sleep." He closes his eyes sagging against the wall even more.

"Blake!"

He opens his eyes looking at Casey who just called out his name.

"What?" He asks grouchily glaring at him.

Well he's an angry person in the morning.

"We want yogurt!" Casey says very loudly causing Blake's glare to deepen,mug Casey doesn't back down.

Blake turns his back heading up the stairs, "No!" He calls back to Casey before disappearing around the corner Into the hallway.

"Allison." Casey turns to me sticking out his bottom lip. He actually looks innocent, and sweet.

I let out a sigh, "Okay, go get dressed." I tell him running a hand through my hair. He gives me a smile before running off to his room to get dress.

I walk up the stairs to the twins room, they're already awake and watching TV in their beds. "We're going to get yogurt." I tell them and they immediately hop out of their beds.

I go through their drawers looking for them something to wear. "Alli." I feel a tugging on my shirt and turn to see Lacey looking at me with sad eyes.

I stop going through the clothes and squat to her level, "What is it Lace?" I ask ruffling her hair.

"Blake made us." She says and I pull my eyebrows together in confusion.

"What did Blake make you do?" I ask.

"Be bad." Macey says and she looks sad just like Macey "We're sorry." She looks at the ground and Lacey looks like she's about to cry.

I try to figure out what they're talking about and realize that's why they were bad yesterday. I thought they were just being bad, but Blake made them act up, while he was off running "errands" that damn devil.

I put on a fake smile, "It's okay," I say giving them both a hug to cheer them up. An idea comes to me and I smirk, "Look, I want you to go wake up Blake as loud as you can. Scream, jump on him, do whatever it takes, until he's up, okay?"

They both nod enthusiastically before running off to Blake's room.

That stupid jerk.

How dare he make the children be bratz.... Now that I think of it, he wasn't to fond of my date with Daniel. That son of a bitch. He sabotaged my whole date.

Oh he's gonna pay.

"Allison, what the hell?" Speak of the devil, "Why did Lacey and Macey come to my room sounding like a herd of elephants?" Blake's leaning against the door frame with his arms crossed over his chest.

"Get dressed, we're going to get yogurt." I tell him going back to picking out the twins's clothes, "And if you try going back to sleep I'll just get them to wake you up again." I say not even bothering to glance up at him.

I hear him let out a grunt before he leaves the room.

Oh boy, he has no idea how horrible today is going to be for him.

"Allison, I don't see why in the hell we couldn't just take my car here." Blake complains opening the door to the yogurt place. We walked all the way from Rachel's house to here, it's about a 30 minute walk and the twins were tired writhing the first 5 minutes so Blake had to pick them up and alternate every couple of minutes. I knew they would be tired when I said that we should walk.

"Fresh air helps hangovers," I say in amusement, "Especially when the sun is out."

Blake is probably about to die from the sun right now since he has a horrible hangover. "You are so evil." He mutters but I can still hear him, and I let out a chuckle.

"Okay what do you guys want?" I ask the kids when we get over to the yogurt machines that are spread along the walls each containing different favors.

"Strawberry." Macey says while Lacey Says, "Chocolate."

"I want vanilla," Casey says already grabbing one of the cups that you place the yogurt in, and going to the Vanilla machine. He can barely reach the handle so he stands on his tippy toes. I roll my eyes and grab a cup for Macey and Lacey both.

I fill the cups up to the top knowing that its way to much for them.

"Can I get toppings?" Casey asks and I notice Blake sitting at one of the tables with his head down.

"Sure, get as many as you want." I encourage him with a smirk on my face.

I grab a cup for myself filling it to the top with cookies and cream yogurt. At the toppings are I cover it in CoolWhip before putting Oreos and chocolate syrup on the top of that.

The worker behind the cash register gestures for us to put our cups on top of the scale to see how much it cost. The cost depends on the weight so the more you get the more it costs. Blake walks over to us with his arms folded over his chest.

"Twenty three, fourty nine," The worker tells us holding out his hand for the money.

I turn to Blake putting on a sad face, "I left my money at home, can you pay for it?"

Blake frowns at me muttering something under his breath, but he pulls his wallet out of his pocket and passes over a twenty and a ten to the man. I catch a glimpse of the inside of his wallet, seeing that he has a bunch of money. I'm not even sure how he gets that thing to close. The last time I checked he doesn't have a job, and I'm pretty sure Beatrice isn't supplying him with that much money. Deciding its none of my business I grab my yogurt off the scale pushing Macey and Lacey in front of me so I can keep an eye on them.

We start heading towards the exit, "We're not staying here?" Blake asks causing the frown that was already on his face to deepen.

"Of course not, why waste a sunny day spending it indoors." I tell him knowing he's just trying to avoid the sun because of his hangover. In reality I really don't care too much for the heat but if it pisses Blake off I'm all for it.

Blake grumbles something following us outside. From where we stand I can see that the park is only some yards away so I start walking in that direction. When we get to the park Casey is done with his yogurt already but the twins still have a lot. Instead of sitting down and eating the rest they take off to the playground.

I sit down on one of the benches in the shade under a big tree.Blake sits down next to me but not that close. I can see Macey and Lacey on the see saw while Casey is on the swings.

"Why are you touring me?" Blake asks catching me off guard.

"What are you talking about?" I ask trying to sound innocent as I avoid his eyes.

I hear him shift next to me, "Sweetcheeks, I'm not stupid, you're trying to torture me, why?" He asks and I can feel his stare burning a hole into the side of my head.

"Why did you make the kids ruin my date?" I ask crossing my arms over my chest finally turning to face him.

"I don't know what your talking about." He says.

"Well I don't know what you're talking about." I shoot back at him turning around to face the park again.

We sit in silence while I eat my yogurt.

"Daniel's a jerk." Blake finally says causing me to look at him.

"What are you taking about?" I question.

"That's why I told the kids to run around, and give you hell." He admits looking out at the park.

"So you called yourself looking out for me?" I am in disbelief.

"Yea, in a way." He says with a shrug of his shoulders.

"And I believe this why?"

"I don't know," He says finally facing me, "It's up to you to believe me or not," He reaches out taking my yogurt from me and putting a spoonful into his mouth.

"Blake!" I shriek reaching for the yogurt but he snatches it back from me and smirks.

"What's the magic word, Bambi?"

"I'm going to kill you." I threaten for the millionth time.

"I said word, not four words." He grins standing up and holding the ice cream over his head so I can't reach it.

"Blake just me the yogurt!"

He turns around and starts running away with my yogurt, and I run after him. Being on the basketball and soccer team I'm not tired but I don't feel like chasing him, especially since he's pretty fast.

We end up back at the bench we were sitting on that the twins yogurt is still sitting on. "Maybe you should give up Bambi." Blake says smiling at me from behind the bench since I'm in front of it. He puts another spoonful in his mouth, "Hmmm, you have good taste." He teases before flicking yogurt at me.

He did not just do that.

I grab one of the twins's yogurt chucking it at Blake, and laughing when it hits him dead in the chest ruining his shirt. "This is polo, do you know how much it cost me." He says examining the shirt and I take that as my chance to attack him.

Wrong idea.

Just as I'm standing in front of him he looks at me with a smirk and dumps my yogurt on the top of my head. My scalp begins to get wet and cold and I look at Blake in shock while he smirks at me. I grab the remaining yogurt cup trying to pour it on his head but since he's too tall I end up pouring it down his neck and it stains the rest of his shirt.

"I'll be getting my revenge, Darling." He tells me with his arms crossed over his chest.

"Wouldn't have it any other way Drayton," I tell him before stomping over to the playground to get the kids.

"It's time to go," I tell them when I have all three of them gathered up.

"No, I don't want to go." Casey complains stomping his feet while crossing his arms over his chest.

"We'll you don't have an option." I tell him just as the twins start composing too.

Oh Lord.

"Look this isn't optional," I tell them squatting to their level.

Cash sticks his tongue out at me before running back over to the playground. The twins do the same thing as. Heir brother also running off.

I seriously don't have time for this.

I walk over to Blake frowning, "Can you go get those damn demons?" I complain.

"Nah," He says and My scowl deepens, "Will's coming to watch them." He quickly tells me.

We only have to wait for a little bit before Will comes, surprisingly Jasmine's with him. How in the hell did that happen? N, how are they both alive? Usually those two can't be in the room together for more than thirty seconds.

Jasmine gives me a look letting me know not to even ask so I don't. Blake and I began walking to Rachel's house and he's walking behind me since I'm walking pretty fast.

I feel arms engulf me and a cold wetness on my back before I hear chuckling. "I'm going to seriously kill you one of these days Drayton!" I exclaim pushing Blake off of me.

Great.

Now not only is my hair wet but also my back, and it's all Blake's fault.

As usual.

I basically power walk home and I can hear Blake laughing the whole way. When we get to the house I go straight up to my guest room grabbing my suitcase.

Crap.

The only day clothes that I have left are for tommorow.

Letting out a sigh I walk down to Blake's guest room hoping he has on a shirt this time. Okay, well maybe I'm hoping he doesn't have on a shirt.

I push open the door not even bothering to knocking, finding Blake -with a shirt on- going through his suit case. When I walk in he turns his head to look at me, "Did you come back for round two of last night?" He asks going back o his suitcase, which is a relief. Since I'm pretty sure I'm blushing.

"I'm out of day clothes," I tell him leaning against the door frame trying to compose myself, "Do you have anything I can bor--." My sentence is cut off when something hits me in the face.

Ouch.

I remove the thing from my face seeing that its a white T-Shirt. Something else hits me and I see that it's black basketball shorts,"Well thanks." I say sarcastically throwing the clothes over my shoulder.

He turns to look at me with a smirk on his face and I know he's going to say something stupid, "Well you could just walk around the house nude, I'm pretty sure I would enjoy that." He says smiling as though that's going to actually happen.

I reach down and take off my shoe throwing it at him, "Ow," He says rubbing the side of his head before looking at me with amusement in his eyes.

"Blake," I say backing away from him as he walks towards me.

"Where do you think your going Bambi?" He asks as his steps become faster and I start running away from him.

Me and Blake in a house together Alone, and he's chasing after me.

Oh, this can't possibly be good.

Chapter 13

I shiver as Blake takes off my top and throws it across the room. The cold air hits me, but turning the air conditioner off would mean stopping what we're doing right now. As much as I despise Blake I have to admit that I don't want that to happen.

My hands slip under his shirt and touch his rock hard abs. His skin is burning up and I want to feel it against mine so I pull up the he, of it. Noticing what I'm trying to do Blake helps me and throws his shirt in a corner when we finally manage to get it off our lips barely moving from each others.

15 MINUTES EARLIER

"Allison!" Blake calls out as he walks around the house looking for me.

I'm currently hiding under Casey's bed which is cramped and full of dust. I really regret throwing that shoe at Blake. Every since then Blake has been chasing after me and I know if he gets me it isn't going to be too good. Luckily I managed to throw his clothes that he'd let me borrow at him, and he had to stop, giving me time to hide.

"You can't hide for long, you may as well come out!" He calls out and I can hear his footsteps right outside of Casey's room.

Maybe he'll turn around.

I hear the knob being turned before Blake's footsteps are in the room.

Or not.

I can see his feet from under the bed and I began to panic. I roll to the opposite side of where he's at as a plan forms in my mind. I watch as his feet are right by the bed. Just as he leans down to look under the bed I run from my side easily escaping him.

"Allison!" He calls out again and I know he saw me.

I run through the house before running into his guest bed room and locking the door behind me. I hear him when he reaches he door and surprisingly he doesn't try to open it, "Allison, I'm going to give you ten seconds to open the door."

I don't respond I simply sit on his bed smiling to myself since he can't get in.

That idiot.

"One." He calls out.

I take off my remaining shoe throwing it on the ground.

"Two!"

I lean back on the bed.

"Three!"

I find his TV remote.

"Four!"

I start scrolling through the stations.

"Five!"

Hmm, Twilight's on.

"Six"

I watch as Edward rips James's body to streds and Bella shivers on the floor like a wimp. I bet turning into a vampire doesn't even hurt that bad.

"Nine!" Blake calls out louder interrupting my thoughts.

I'd stop even listening to him count since its pointless, because the door is locked.

"Ten!"

Ha, dumb jerk, you can't eve-

Blake interrupts my thoughts yet again when he opens the door with a grin on his face to my utter surprise.

I hop off the bed and try to get away from him but its too late he already has me laying back on the bed while hovering over me. "Did I mention that the door doesn't lock, Casey broke it."

Shit.

This is why I don't like Casey, he's ruining my life even when he's not around.

"So Sweetcheeks are you going to apologize?" His warm breath blows on my neck causing tingles all over my body.

I can't even open my mouth to talk for two reasons. The first being because I'm too damn stubborn, and the second because I really don't want him to get off of me.

"So I take that as a no," he says kissing my neck causing me to shiver. He leans his head back to look me in the eyes, "Last chance Sweetcheeks." There's a challenge in his eyes that makes me keep my mouth shut.

Plus, I just may like this punishment.

PRESENT TIME

Our lips move together in a synchronized motion before Blake's tongue slides across my lips trying to enter. I open my mouth and our lips start to tangle. I roll us over so I'm now on top and my hair starts to hang down brushing Blake's chest. One of Blake's hands reaches out and pushes my hair behind my ear on one of my shoulders. He then lets both of his hands hold my waist before flipping us over again.

He starts to run his hand along the bare sides of my stomach before reaching for the straps of my bras. I'm not subconscious of my body or anything, hell I let him take my shirt off which I rarely let a boy do when making out. But, I'm not so sure about taking my bra off, I mean it's not like we're going to do anything besides make out.

Fortunately his hands leave my bra, but they go do down to the button of my jeans, which isn't much better. Nu uh, if he's going take off my pants, he has to take his off.

"Pants off for pants off," I mumble trying to use the least words I can.

Blake understands what I'm trying to say so he slips his pants off before taking mine off.

This isn't too bad since a lot of guys have seen me in a bikini which is basically bra and panties.

What is bad though is that Blake seems intent on getting my bra and panties off, which isn't going to happen.

"Blake," I groan out as he kisses my neck while his hands fumble with my bra.

"Okay," he mumbles understanding what I'm hinting at and he removes his hands from my undergarments.

Ding.

The doorbell down stairs rings and we both jump apart. Well more like reluctantly jump apart.

Shit.

We've got to stop doing this.

Blake glances at me before throwing me some of his clothes as he starts to get dressed. "I'll get the door," He says when he has his pants back on.

He doesn't seem like his usual arrogant self, and he's not teasing me about what just happened which is weird.

"Okay," is all I can say an I watch as he leaves the room closing the door behind him.

I sit down on the bed putting my head in my hands.

I'm so screwed up its pitiful.

One moment I can't stand Blake and the next I come close to sleeping with him. This is ridiculous.

With a sigh I put on the shirt Blake gave me, and his basketball shorts which are too big for me. I leave the room and jog down the stairs to see who was at the door. I know who it is before I reach the living room because I can here the loud arguing.

I walk in the living to see the kids, Jasmine, and Will. To say that I'm shocked at the sight in front of me is an understatement. "What in the hell did you two do?" I ask Will and Jasmine who are both covered in mud.

"Well," Jasmine says and I can tell Blake -who's standing by the kids- also wants to know what happened, "It started raining so we were getting the kids together when Will tripped right Into a fu-" She cuts herself off as she glances at the kids, "Into a mud pile." She says, "So I pulled him in and then you know stuff happened."

Will shakes his head, "No, she's lying, that is not what happened." He tells us glaring at her, "I accidentally tripped her and when I went to help her up she threw me in." He justifies himself and I can't help but laugh.

"You think this is funny?" Jasmine asks glaring at me.

"Yes," Blake says and he's also laughing.

Will frowns at us, "And Allison why do you have Blake's clothes on, and Blake why don't you have a shirt on?" He asks as if he knows a secret.

Shit.

Think of A Lie ALLISON.

Think of a really good one.

"We got into the yogurt fight you know, and Allison didn't have extra clothes so I let her borrow some." Blake lies smoothly, sitting down on the couch casually.

Thank god he's a good liar.

"Really, and Blake you didn't answer the question about your shirt." Jasmine points out choosing the wrong time to be on Will's side.

"I had just gotten done taking a shower and was about to put my shirt on when y'all rung the doorbell," He spits out another lie. Shrugging his shoulders casually. "You guys should probably go home and clean up." He suggests.

Reluctantly, Will and Jasmine end up leaving but from the look on their faces I know they're still suspicious.

Not good.

Chapter 14

When Monday comes I'm relieved for a couple of reasons. The first being that I'm finally done avoiding Blake in the same house. Rachel didn't get back until last night, and I've been avoiding Blake every since the hot make out. I really need to get a hold of my hormones when I'm around him. So basically for the rest of the weekend I hid in my guest bed room only occasionally coming out too check of the kids. Surprisingly Blake didn't try to tease me or even bother me for that mater. It's as if he's intent on staying away from me too. Which is perfectly fine with me. Fortunately, mom let me drive her car to school this morning and told Beatrice to tell Blake I didn't need a ride.

Another reason why I'm happy that its Monday is because I get to see Daniel, and try to apologize. I mean he can't even possibility be that mad, it's not like we're dating, plus, I can kiss who ever I want.

Now the reason that I even come to school period, we have a scrimmage soccer game today against Evangel (a catholic school.) This is the first game of the season and even though is not really going on our record its always fun, and people always show up. Our real season doesn't start for a couple of weeks. We also get to get out of class all day, it shows just how sports crazy our school is. So we'll basically spend today chilling in the gym and playing around. We'll probably practice a little but coach won't work us too hard until before the game.

"You ready?"Jasmine asks walking up to me while texting on her phone.

"Yeap," I tell her thumping her forehead so she'll stop texting, she glares at me rubbing her head before we start to walk to the gym. "So how was your weekend, well the rest of it?" I ask her opening the gym door.

She walks into the gym ahead of me and shrugs her shoulders, "It was okay, and yours, did you sleep with Blake again?"

My mouth drops open and I stop walking, when she realizes I stopped she turns around grinning at me, "Someone looks guilty." Before I can even reply she turns around and starts walking again.

"Hey!" I call out jogging to catch up with her, once I reach her I start walking again, "I did not sleep with Blake." I tell her.

"Which time?" She asks as we head to the girls locker room.

"There was no times." I tell her, "I have never slept with Blake and don't plan on it."

"Well that part isn't a lie, but I don't believe your story about what happened Saturday." She tells me and I don't get a chance to tell her what actually happened since we're in the locker room with the rest of the team now. All three of our coaches are here, Coach Lee, Coach Miles, and Coach May.

"Finally you two are here," Coach Lee (our head coach) says when we walk in to sit on the benches with everyone else. We take a seat before coach starts to speak, "Girls, I know today is just suppose to be a pre season game but we're going to act like its the championship ladies!" He gets louder as he continues to talk. I start tuning him out because honestly it's hours before the game and he's already yelling so I know that it's going to get much worst later, so why listen now. I don't need him to be running up my blood pressure or anything.

After coach goes on and on about whatever he's talking about he dismisses us to the stage of the gym to do whatever we want. The stage in the gym is right behind the basketball goal and can be seen from the basketball court and bleachers, but today coach has the curtains pulled so no one can see us.

"Man you know tonight he's going to bitch like crazy."Jasmine says sitting next to me on the wooden floor of the stage.

"I know," I tell her shaking my head, "but I'm not going to listen to him, that's why I got these babies." I show her my new blue earbuds that I bought just for the season. I could've simply used some of my old ones but they wouldn't have been loud enough to drown him out.

"Dude, I bought those too, mine are purple though," She says pulling out her earbuds that are almost identical to mine.

"Now we just have to keep our hoodies on, and we'll be fine." I say high fiving her.

When it's our P.E. hour Jasmine begs Coach Lee to let us go play volleyball. As you can probably guess I don't beg to play that killing sport I simply shake my head at Coach Lee from behind Jasmine's back hoping he understands that I don't want to play. Why must I play if I don't want to, you ask. Well if Jasmine plays its just like girl code that I go and play with her.

"Okay, but I don't care if the ball hits you in the head harder than a fret train, you'll still be playing in the game, concussion and all." He finally gives in and I know he's dead serious about the concussion part even though I'm not sure if you can get one from a volleyball.

"Thanks, Coach." Jasmine says before grabbing my hand and pulling me down the stairs of the stage so we can go in the gym. Our actual PE coach, coach Willis tells us we don't have to dress out since it will make no sense because we're already in our soccer warm up clothes.

While everyone else is getting dressed out we start volleying the ball to each other from opposite sides of the net. You see, this I can handle but when there's a lot of people and the ball is flying at 120 miles hour, then I'll start hiding behind everyone.

The boys come out of the locker room before the girls, as usual. I have no idea how they get dressed that fast. The seniors and juniors come over to the net that we're at while the lower class men go to the other net. Playing with a lot of people is bad but playing with a lot of boys is horrible so I go to hide behind a tall dude who I know is pretty good and won't let me get hit.

"Shit," I say before rubbing the back Of my head.Something hit me in the back of my effing head, and it hurts like a son of a bitch.

"What the fu-" I catch myself and don't finish my sentence when I see Coach Willis raise a brow at me just as she's about to go into her office. I turn around to see Mercedes smirking and I know that whore hit me in the back of the head on purpose. Shit, I didn't even know that the girls were out of the locker room.

I look to see that the only coaches that are out are at the other end of the gym which is good because I'm about to send this bitch flying across Mars and I don't need anyone getting in my way.

"You bitch," is the first words out of my mouth as I start running towards her. She looks like she's scared and starts backing away. "Oh what so now your scared?" I ask going to swing at her face but somebody grabs me around my waist pulling me away from Mercedes and spinning me around so I can't hit her.

As I'm still cussing and trying to hit Mercedes the person starts to pull me out of the gym, and I pray to god that the person isn't a coach. I know my face is red from anger and my body is burning up.

"Please calm down Allison," I hear Jasmine say when we're outside. Whoever grabbed me is still holding me and I can feel that there well muscled. Jasmine appears in front of me shaking her head, "Babe, you have got to calm down."

"No, I've got to go fuck up Mercedes," I say trying to break free from the person holding me. I hear the gym door open and feel the person holding me grips loosen so I take that as my chance and break free.

Ha, no one can hold me d-.

I break off from my thoughts as someone grabs me just as I'm about to go in the gym. I look up to see Blake shaking his head at me, "Let me go, Blake!" I yell pounding on his chest before he grabs my hands and pins them behind my back. He manages to make me walk back to where Jasmine is along with Will. I guess that's who was holding me down, I never would have thought that Will is that well built.

"Allison, calm down if you lay a hand on Mercedes you won't be playing in the game tonight." Jasmine warns, "Catch that whore after school but don't do it right now."

"No, I already don't like her and then she had the nerve to hit me in the back of the fucking head."

"Dang girl, you sure do cuss a lot when your mad." Will says leaning against the wall cussing Jasmine to send him a glare.

"You need to cool off." Jasmine says pulling out her phone to I guess check the time, "Blake maybe you should take Allison away from the school for a while." She suggests, "We don't have to start getting ready for the game for some hours."

What the hell is she thinking.

"It's gonna be a while before she calms down, I know her, and the last time something like this happened I thought I was going to have to lock her in my trunk."

"Alright," I hear Blake say and I can feel the vibration of his chest against my back.

"Aright nothing," I complain, "This is what's going to happen your going to let me go in there and kick Mercedes ass." I say but Blake is already dragging me to his car.

"Bye Honey!" Jasmine calls out waving at me with a smirk on her face. That loser, what kind of best friend is she.

Blake unlocks his car while still holding me, he opens the passenger door and throws me in. He does something to the door before closing it. Instead of being like those idiots who try to run while their capturer is outside I wait for Blake to get in before trying to make a run. As soon as Blake closes his door after getting in, I try to open the door, but it won't budge.

Damn it.

"Child locks sure are a miracle, huh?" Blake says with a smirk on his face as he pulls out of the school parking lot. "So where do you suggest we go?" He asks with that smirk still on his face, and I know he's back to annoying me. I guess he's completely over this weekend, and to think I thought he was going to be civilized for a while.

"You know that new arcade place just opened up, and I here they have good food." He says in a happy voice.

"Arcades are for children," I tell him looking out the window seeing that Blake is doing at least 70 in a 45 speed zone. "Slow down, dammit."

"Will's right, you do curse a lot when your mad." He says not slowing down his speed one bit.

"I thought that you were done aggravating me."

From the corner of my eye I see him glance at me, there's a weird look on his face before he turns his eyes back to the road. "Of course not." He says but he doesn't sound as cheerful as he was just a while ago.

Weird.

The car makes a sharp turn into a parking lot and I read the neon sign above the building "Winter's Cade." I guess 'Cade' is the abbreviation for arcade since this is probably the place Blake was talking about. The building is huge, it looks like its even a two story, this is the biggest arcade I've ever seen, my goodness.

"You seriously did not bring me to an arcade." I say bitterly as the car comes to a stop.

"Of course I did," He says taking the key out of the ignition and getting out without waiting for me.

With a sigh I try to open my door forgetting about the child lock. Just as I remember, Blake opens my door holding it open for me. For some reason my cheeks heat up and I know I'm blushing. It's Blake, and he simply opened the door for me because I couldn't. It's nothing special.

I look down at the ground trying to hide my face as I get out of the car. Blake shuts the door behind me and leads me inside the building.

On the inside the arcade is basically glow in the dark so when we first walk in I'm shocked. There's no lights on but all of the games are lit up. There's only a handful of people here since school is going on right now, but theres a few adults, and kids too young for school. I'm not even sure how many games there is since there's so many but I know they have a shooting game, basketball, driving games, and a lot of other stuff.

"Come on," Blake says grabbing my hand which surprises me. Still kind of in shock I let him lead me through some double doors in the back of the arcade. In this room there's actually lights on and a lot of tables for people to eat at. There's a place to order food that's kind of set up like a bar so you can sit down there also. The walls are white, while the floor is a blueberry blue. A couple of people are sitting at the tables eating and there's a woman behind the bar like setup.

Blake leads me to where the woman is and when she sees him her face lights up. "Blake!" She exclaims with a huge smile.

She looks to be in her late forties with hair the color of chocolate, and blue eyes. "Miranda," Blake says to the woman with a smile, "This is Allison, Allison this is Miranda." He introduces us.

"Hey there Sweetie," She greets me as if we've known each other for for ever.

"Hi," I say giving her a polite smile even though I'm still pissed off about earlier.

"Blake you didn't let me know that you had such a pretty girlfriend." She says looking down at our hands that are still locked together.

"Oh, uh well we're not together." He tells her casually letting my hand go.

Miranda's face falls for a second before it lights up again, "Whatever you say." By the way she says it I can tell she doesn't believe us but she doesn't push it.

"Do you two want anything to eat?" She asks.

"Nah, we'll get something later." Blake tells her.

"Alright, well here," She says passing him a card that she takes from under the counter. From what I can tell it looks like a credit card but I don't think that's what it is.

"Thank you," Blake says shoving the card into his pocket, "We'll be back before we leave." He tells her and with that we leave Miranda to do something else.

Blake opens the double doors again and we're back in the dark, "What game do you want to play first?" He asks me.

I look around before deciding on playing a shooting game. We walk over to it and Blake takes the little card out of his pocket sliding it through a slot on the game. Well that's what it goes to. He watches as I play the game but he doesn't join in. When I shoot the last zombie on the screen we go to another game.

I don't know how many games Blake and I have played, or how long we've been here but I feel much calmer, and I'm actually enjoying myself.

"I totally kicked your ass." I tell Blake as our game of air hockey ends.

"Oh shut up," he says slinging an arm over my shoulder as we walk back to the cafe.

"You know it's true," I tell him reaching over my chest with my right hand to poke him, he simply laughs and opens the door to the cafe.

"I see you two are back." Miranda says leaning on the counter and watching us.

"Yeap," He says popping the 'p', he drops his arm from my shoulder so we can sit down and I suddenly feel like something's missing but I don't let it show.

We sit on the little bar stools and Miranda stands in front of us on the opposite side of the counter. "So what can I get you two drink and eat?"

"Uh do you have A menu?" I ask since I've never been here before now.

"Just get her a cheeseburger, I'll take a monte cristo." Blake tells Miranda, ordering both mine and his food.

"Okay, and to drink?"

"Do you have Strawberry milkshakes?" I ask her and she nods, "Okay I'll have that."

She looks at Blake waiting for his drink.

"I'll just have an Oreo malt."he tells her and she goes through some double doors behind the bar that I'm guessing leads to the kitchen.

"Hey is this place a two story?" I ask him remembering that when we first got here it looked like a two story.

Blake looks at me, "Yea, the upstairs part is a club at night time." He says.

"Really?" I ask just as Miranda comes back with our drinks before going back in the kitchen, "So at night time the adults party while the kids play in the arcade?"

Blake nods his head, "Basically, but the arcade closes early before all the crazy people come out, and there's two different entrances." He explains to me, "You can't even go from the club to the arcade and there's usually security working."

"How do you know all of this?" I ask and he simply shrugs his shoulders. Not ungrateful me an answer.

Miranda appears with our food and my burger is huge, she sits it down in front of me with a smile. I look at Blake's page trying to figure out what in the heck he's eating. It's like these fried triangle things but there's something on the inside, and it smells amazing, like a funnel cake.

"What's that?" I ask him as he takes a bite of one of them.

He finishes chewing his food before answering, "A monte cristo," he tells me.

"I already knew that," I tell him with a frown as I take a bite out of my burger. It tastes amazing the seasoning on ip the burger is spicy but not too hot, it's just right. There's a little ketchup and mustard, the cheese is hot too, making me wonder if they have a regular unspicy burger.

"Well you asked what it was and I told you." He says going back to his annoying self.

"You know what I mean," I say getting frustrated.

Blake smirks knowing he already made me mad, "It's a fried sandwich," He says passing me a piece that he's already bitten off of.

"Uh, no thanks, there's no telling what I can catch from you."

"I only had mono once, and that was forever ago," He says seriously glancing at me. I stare at him with my mouth open, "I'm joking," he says chuckling, I punch his shoulder before looking at the food skeptically.

Blake lets out a sigh picking up my burger and taking a huge bite, I stare at him in shock. That thing, did not just bite my burger, "Look now if you had anything I have it, it's only fair if you take the same risk." He says with a shrug.

"I don't have anything that you can catch," I mumble, finally giving in I take a bite of the sandwich and boy is it good. If subway would sell these things they'd make so much money.

"Good, huh?" Blake says smirking at me.

"It's okay," I say and we both know I'm lying.

After we're done eating our food Blake decides to take me back to school to join the rest of the soccer team. I still want to beat the spit out of Mercedes but I think I'll let it wait. Blake and I must've been gone for a good while because its only an hour left before the game. The game today is a home one so its going to be at our stadium that's only down the street.

Instead of taking me to the school like originally planned, Blake drops me off at the stadium. He tells me he's going to stay for the game so he walks me down to the stadium. Well honestly it isn't really a stadium, its just the soccer field which is huge and bleachers on one side for the audience. I think at the most it can hold 150 people, but usually people bring their own fold up chairs and sit along the sides of the fields. On the other side of the field there's two benches for the teams and coaches. What possessed them to put two opposing teams next to each other, I have no idea.

"Alright,"Blake says rubbing the back of his neck awkwardly before looking at me with a nervous look, it's actually cute, "Well I'm going to go wait for the game to start."he says as if he's not sure if that's what he should do.

"Okay," I say realizing I sound just as awkward as him, "Well, bye." I tell him before walking over to where my team mates are chilling on the benches. Well half the team is sitting on the benches while the other half are sitting on the ground and standing up, since the genius who made the bleachers made it for eight people to sit on.

"Well hey Boo," Jasmine says when I walk over to where she is.

"Hey," I say giving her a smile.

"You seem happy now, and I saw that little cute awkward thing with Blake." She says with a mischievous smile on her face.

"I don't know what you're talking about," I say sitting on the ground with her.

"Mm hmm," She says rolling her eyes.

A whistle blows and I turn to see Coach Lee standing with his clip board, "Alright girls, take a lap." He says and I swear for two reasons: I just say down, and a lap around this field is fucking exhausting.

With a sigh I stand up and Jasmine and I start jogging together around the field. I see no point in running this big ass field before a game, that's just plain out tiring. I get tired before the game even starts when we do this crap, and do you know what the other teams do? Sit and Watch. Their freaking coaches don't make them do all this running.

We finally complete our lap and we're both breathing a little hard, like everyone else. "Hey Allison!" Coach calls out and I turn to look at him, "Take another lap." He says.

"What?" This idiot has lost his mind, "Why?"

"Well because you almost got into a fight at school, yes I know about that, and you didn't ride with the team, not to mention you skipped the rest of school." He says with a shake of his, "And now your going to run a third one for questioning me, so get to it." He blows his whistle, "Everyone else go work on passing drills."

Seriously, screw my life.

Chapter 15

"Darling, get your head in the game!" Coach yells at me from the sidelines as he bangs his hands on his clipboard.

He's effing up my concentration even worst than it already was. Coach stuck me as starting forward, which I'm pretty good at. The only problem is he stuck his daughter -Megan- in as the other forward. Let me start by saying Megan is horrible, the only reason she made the team is because of her father. She's not aggressive enough, every time she gets the ball the other team steals it from her. She's horrible at passing so I have to always run to it since it never makes it to me. So coach is hollering at me when his daughter is the one fucking up the game.

Like now, Megan has the ball and she's trying to dribble but she's kicking it too far so a defender is already on her. The defender kicks the ball back all the way to our midfield and I'm happy to see that Jasmine now has the ball. She dribbles up the field pass defenders, as I run towards the goal.

"Jaz!!" I call out and she glances at me before sending the ball flying at me. She kicked the ball so hard I'm pretty sure that the maker of soccer balls felt it. When the ball is still in the air but by me, I take a one touch kick sending it right at the goal. The goalie tries to catch it but I kicked it too high or her to grab.

The bleachers go wild as I make the first goal of the season, and game. Jasmine high fives me when I get back to the middle of the field. "That's what I'm talking about, girl." She says slapping me on the back.

Once every is lined back up in their positions the ref blows the whistle signaling the kick off. It's Evangel's kick now, since our team just scored. Their middle forward kicks the ball upfield just as their outside forward runs up to the ball. I watch as one of our defenders takes the ball and kicks it up to one of our midfielders -Jonah.- Jonah passes the ball to me and I run upfield getting around their midfield. I hear Megan calling for the ball but of course I don't pass it to her. I see Jasmine taking the middle of the field so I pass it to her and she ends up scoring.

"Darling!" Coach yells as we line up again, "What was that?" He continues to yell at me, "Megan was open!"

I glance at him to see that he's pissed but I ignore him as the ref blows the whistle again. Evangel ends up scoring, finally, and now it's our turn to kick the ball upfield. I take the kick and kick it softly, just enough to get to Megan, hopefully she'll get it.

Wrong, a midfielder takes the ball away from her. I let out a sigh, getting pissed off, I take the ball from the midfielder as adrenaline pumps through my body. Just as I'm about to kick the ball in the goal I'm roughly shoved to the ground by a defender on the other team. I hear the whistle as the ref blows it signaling a penalty kick. Since it was in the penalty kick the other teams defense can't even try to block the shot.

"Come on Ali Babe!" Jasmine yells and everyone in the bleachers starts to cheer me on.

With a deep breath I step behind the ball where the ref has placed it. The skinny little goalie looks kind of worried and wipes her hands off on her shorts.

"Go Sweetcheeks!" I hear someone yell and I know without looking who it is.

I take the kick and the ball goes into the corner of the goal. In all honestly I don't even think the goalie tried to block the shot. I turn to the bleachers to see Blake giving me a thumbs up, while Will is waving at me. I smile and jog back to the center of the field. Jasmine high fives me and the game continues on.

The game ends up being a complete blowout with a score of 12-4.

"That's what I'm talking about ladies!" Coach Miles says high fiving some of us as we come off the field. "Especially you Darling." He says with a genuine smile as he pats me on the back.

I give him a smile before collapsing on the ground to catch my breath. My chest feels like its going to cave in its burning so bad. Every breath that I takes causes pain in my chest. Even though I'm well conditioned I know that I overworked myself tonight. Plus this is the first game of the season, so of course it's the roughest on me.

"Allison are you okay?" Jasmine asks sitting on the ground next to me and she's breathing hard too.

I give her a forced smile, "Peachy," I tell her, "Are you okay?" I ask with a raised eyebrow since it looks like she's about to faint.

She gives me a thumbs up just as coach Lee starts to give some kind of speech. "Hey Freshy!" Jasmine calls out to one of the freshman. "Bring us something to drink."

"And candy!" I call out as she starts to jog to the concession stand.

The freshmen are all on the JV team so they didn't play tonight but its required that they come to our games. They basically cater to everyone on the varsity team, and are our groupies. I remember those days, I'm pretty sure Jasmine got into a fight with one of the varsity players when she told Jasmine to go get her something to drink, and to make it snappy. I think Jasmine was cool with it until she heard the girl say something about "the help" then all hell broke loose.

"Allison, Jasmine, get your butts off the ground and get over here!" Coach yells since we're the only people on the team that aren't in the huddle where he's speaking.

He's got to be out of his damn mind. We just played for forty minutes straight and now he's complaining about us sitting on the ground.

Jasmine and I exchange looks and I know she's thinking same thing I am.

"Alright then, since you want to be hard headed, give me two laps." He looks at his watch on his wrist, "You have five minutes, or you won't be playing in the next game." He says and I want to punch him in the face so bad.

With a sigh I stand up and stick out a hand to help Jasmine. "Lets go," she says letting out a breath and we start to jog the first lap.

If you've ever seen the size of a soccer field you know it's pretty big. If you've ever played on the field for forty minutes straight you know afterwards you become tired as hell. What you don't know because nobody's ever had a coach as crazy as Coach Lee, is that when you run around the field after a game it's a pain in the ass.

"Two minutes left ladies!" Coach calls out just as we're completing our first lap.

Shit.

Knowing I'm going to feel like shit afterwards I start to sprint and Jasmine does too. We finally finish the laps just in time, and coach has a pissed look on his face still.

"Now, ladies," He says gesturing to Jasmine and I, "Come join the rest of the team, no whining."

With a sigh we both walk over to the team huddle out of breath. "Now that we have the rest of our team." He says eyeing us making it obvious he's calling us out. "This game was an easy one for y'all and you still didn't do that good."

You've got to be kidding me, we did amazing.

"We obviously need to work on a lot of things." He continues to be an asshole and I feel liking punching the crap out of him, "Practice tomorrow after school until five."

Everyone groans at the thought of having to practice for two and a half hours."Don't make me increase it." Coach warns, "Now lady cougars on three." He says sticking his hand out.

Everyone sticks their hands in the middle, "Lady Cougars on three," One of the seniors yells, "One, Two,"

"Lady Cougars," Everyone except Jasmine, and I yell.

I squint my eyes when I see someone jogging over to Jasmine, and I as we pick up our bags. As the person comes closer into our view I realize it's the freshman. "They were just about to close down and there was a couple of people in front of me." She informs us as she passes us the snacks before leaning down on her knees to catch her breath.

Hell, how is she tired? All she did was jog to the concession and back, plus she even got a break in between while waiting. Ugh, this is why freshman disgust me.

"Okay, you can go now." Jasmine says bitterly with her nose turned up.

"You're not going to in burst me?" She asks with a hopeful glint in her eyes.

"You paid for this?" I ask pointing to the snacks with my eyes squinted.

"Yea," She says as if its pretty darn obvious.

Jasmine shakes her head, "Well that's your own fucking fault, and we ain't reimbursing you shit." Jasmine says with her arms crossed over her chest.

The freshman frowns at us, "Why not?"

"Because SlowAss, the team gets everything free from the concession stand. All you had to do was tell them that it was for us." I say with a shake of my head as the girl's mouth drops open. I don't know her name which is part of the reason I called her SlowAss, plus it looks like the name kind of fits her.

Jasmine smirks as she starts munching on her candy, "Bye SlowAss, see you at practice tomorrow." She says obviously not knowing her name either, "And don't forget to pick you lip up off the ground." She says referring to the fact that she still has her mouth hanging open. The girl instantly closes her mouth.

"Bye," I say with a wave before Jasmine and I leave her. We both laugh at the freshmen as we make our way to the bleachers.

Just as we make it to the bleachers a guy comes over and hugs Jasmine. I'm pretty sure I've seen him before at school, and he's not too bad looking with his short black hair and hazel eyes.

"You did good Jaz." He says to her and I roll my eyes. Look like he's one of her new admirers.

I glance around the bleachers before I see Will and Blake. I walk over to the, with Jasmine and her admirer in tow. Blake is wearing his usual annoying smirk, while Will is glaring. I follow the direction of his eyes to see that he's glaring at Jasmine's admirer.

Hmm, I wonder what that's about.

"You did okay," Blake says casually with his smirk still on his face.

"Really, okay?" I question, "I only did okay?"

"Yea," he says, "I'd give you a four out of ten." He informs me as if his opinion matters.

"Know what?" I say as I stick a sour straw in my mouth, "I'm going to act as if you didn't even say that." I tell him as I stuff my snacks into my soccer bag, "Now, lets go because I'm hungry."

"Pushy, are we?" He smirks crossing his arms over his chest, "I wasn't aware of the fact that you were riding with me."

I roll my eyes a him, "Well become aware because you are." I tell him and with those parting words I turn my back on him and start heading towards the parking lot.

"You coming?" I hear Blake ask someone but I'm not sure who.

"Yea." I hear Will answer him, "I'll meet y'all there, just let me know where we're going."

I hear footsteps behind me and know they're walking to the parking lot too.

"I'll take you home." I hear someone say and I'm guessing that its Mr. Admirer.

"O-"

"I'll do it," Will says cutting Jasmine off just as she was about to reply.

Now that I'm curious as to what's going on I turn around. I mean come on, Jasmine and Will are usually arguing their asses off; so for Will to voluntarily take her somewhere, some crazy shit must be going on.

I turn to see Jasmine and Blake both giving Will a crazy look.

Okay, well I guess I'm not the only one finding this kind of weird.

The admirer pulls his eyebrows together in confusion. Obviously he wasn't expecting that either."Nah dude, it's cool, I insist-"

"I insist that you go away and just let me take her home." Will says and Blake begins to crack up when The Admirer looks embarrassed.

I hold back a smile as Will continues to scare off the admirer dude. Blake looks over at me with a smirk on his face and I can't help but to finally start laughing.

With a sigh Jasmine leans aways from the guy, "It's cool Lawson, I-" She's cut off by a snort.

"Your name's Lawson?" Blake asks in shock as he starts to laugh at the dude again, "That name is so lame." He manages to get out in between laughs.

Oh goodness, he did not seriously just tell this dude that his name was lame.

I walk back a couple of steps and grab Blake's arm, "Okay well we're going to go," I say dragging the laughing bug with me and waving goodbye to the other three, "Work out the riding thing." I say with a shake of my head pulling Blake to his car.

By the time we make it to the car Blake has stopped laughing but he has a smile on his face. I roll my eyes at him, getting in the car after he unlocks the door.

"So where to Sweetcheeks?" He asks me as he turns the radio on.

I roll my eyes but decide on not arguing with him and out his nickname for me,

I think about it for a while. I really want a lot of food, so some sort of buffet. An expensive one too since I'm making Blake pay, "How about the grill?"

"That's exp-"

"You know I really wasn't asking you, I was kind of telling you." I cut his last sentence off.

He glances over at me with a glare on his face while I smile at him. He shakes his head at me, "Fine."

I smile just as he turns the radio up even more. I'm pretty sure the people in the car behind us can hear his music.

I turn it down, happy when Blake doesn't protest.

"If you can't hear what I'm trying to say. If you can't read from the same page. Maybe I'm going deaf, maybe I'm going blind. Maybe I'm out of my mind"

Okay, you've got to be kidding me. The first reason being that Blake is singing Robin Thicke. The second reason being he doesn't sound too bad.

I try to avoid looking at him as he sings his heart out. I never would have thought that Blake Drayton can sing. What is the world coming t-.

I'm cut from my thoughts when I feel Blake's finger on my chin as he turns me to face him.

"Okay now he was close, tried to domesticate you. But you're an animal, baby it's in your nature." He sings to me and I can help but blush, especially when I think more about the lyrics.

"Blake focus on the road," I say as I turn my head away from him witch cheeks the color of roses.

I hear him chuckle but he goes back to driving. I'm seriously surprised that we didn't hit anything.

Ha, it would've been weird if I died, and the last thing I heard was sexual lyrics from Blake's mouth.

We finally pull into the parking lot of the grill and I'm happy to get out of the car. Blake and I were too close, and I know he's back to teasing me.

"I texted Blake, and he's on his way." Blake informs me as he walks to my side of the car. He throws his arm over my shoulder and starts to pull me to the front on the restaurant. "We'll wait inside."

He pulls me inside and we sit on one of the benches on the inside that's made for waiting.

The Grill is one of my favorite places to eat because it has everything. They have an Italian section, Mexican Section, Chinese, American, and of course a special place for grilled food. Considering it costs twelve dollars per person to eat, not including drinks, it's really popular.

Tonight though its pretty empty which I'm guessing is because its pretty late.

The door chimes as it opens for more people and I look up to see a frustrated Will. Jasmine is behind him with a pissed look on her face.

Oh this is going to be an eventful dinner.

Chapter 16

"You know all of that is going to go to your stomach." Will says with a frown on his face as he scrunched his nose up at Jasmine's food.

I hold in a laugh as Jasmine flips him off and continues to eat her cupcake. You see Jasmine is we're when it comes to eating. First off she liked to eat her desserts first, which is why her plate is currently full of brownies and cakes. She then eats fruit and makes sure to put cool whip, and ice cream on them, especially her strawberries. Lastly she eats the main food which consists of all meat, just about. She doesn't like vegetables, except broccoli so her plate never really consists of them. Plus, the girl eats like a 400 pound Japanese sumo wrestler; okay, well I can't talk about her there, because I'm the same way.

"I prefer my women petique with huge curves." Will goes on, "And if you keep eating like that, you'll still have the curves, just not the petiqueness." He says gesturing to her stomach and boobs.

Jasmine narrows her eyes at him and shoves a brownie into her mouth. "First off," she says after she's done chewing, "I'm not one of you women, second off all of this food goes to my ass and hips, not my stomach, plus I work out." She tells him before making a show of stuffing her mouth.

"Just disgusting," He says before he jumps and starts to rub his leg. "Did you just kick me?" He asks glaring at Jasmine.

She smirks at him before going back to her food.

So somehow, I ended up sitting next to Will when we were being seated. Jasmine and Blake ended up on a side together; with me sitting across from Blake, and Jasmine and Will sitting across from each other.

"As entertaining as it is to watch you two bicker, I'm going to go get another plate." I tell the two of them standing up from the table before making my way to the buffet line.

I walk over to the Chinese food section looking for some sesame seed chicken. Glancing around I frown when I see that they're out. I feel someone press up behind me and I jump from being startled.

Oh, goodness, I'm going to be kidnapped.

"Looking for this," A husky voice whispers in my ear just as a plate is out in front of my face full of sesame seed chicken.

This ass whole not only is trying to kidnap me but he's also taking all of the chicken. What an ass.

Maybe it's weird that I'm being kidnapped and I'm thinking about chicken, but I don't give a damn. The chicken is my favorite Chinese food and my favorite thing at 'The Grill'.

"Just stay calm and you can have the chicken." The voice says and there's clear amusement. It finally registers in my mind who the ass whole behind me is. I have no idea how I didn't recognize the voice at first.

"You Ass Whole!" I yell turning around and shoving Blake who laughs his butt off. Somehow he manages to still keep the plate in his hand, and continues to laugh.

I see people glance at us as they walk by. We probably look like delinquent teens; partially due to my outburst and Blake's bad boy look.

"Stop laughing, your making a scene." I tell him with a frown on my face.

He glances at my face and continues to laugh before stopping. "If this was a real case scenario you would've been kidnapped." He says with a bright smile on his face.

I glare at him, "Shut up, what else was I suppose to do?" I snap folding my arms over my chest.

"At least tried to escape," He says as if that was pretty obvious.

"Just leave me alone," I tell him, knowing I'm acting like a six year old, but I don care. He scare the living daylight out of me.

"I'm sorry," he says with a smile still on his face, but he looks half sincere. "Here," he tells me holding out the plate of chicken, "it's a peace offering."

I eye the chicken before glancing up at Blake, and repeating the process.

Well, it is sesame seed chicken, and he was just joking.

But then again he's a total ass whole who can't be trusted.

Choosing to forgive him so I can have the sesame seed chicken I snatch it out his hand. A smirk appears on his face since he know he has me won over so I send him a glare before turning my back on him and going back to the table.

I'm not surprised to find Jasmine and Will arguing when I return to the table. You know I use to think that me andBlake had it bad, with the arguing, but these to make us look like best friends.

I do find it weird though that there basically whispering while they're arguing though. Also, they both keep looking around as if they're going to get caught doing something wrong.

"I don't give a damn if he is just a friend.." Will says but once he sees me lets the sentence trail off. There's a worried look on his face for a second but it returns back to normal.

"Oh hey Allison," He says as if everything is normal but I can tell that he's faking.

Jasmine shoots him a glare before stuffing a piece of what looks like chocolate cake in her mouth. "I'm going to go get something else." Will says in a rush scooting out of the booth before I can sit down. Once he's out I sit down sliding into his spot so I'm across from Jasmine.

Jasmine diverts her eyes away from me as she eats her sweets. "So you're not going to tell me what that was about?" I ask watching her curiously.

She glances at me for a second before looking down at her plate, "Nope," she says popping the 'p' before looking up and sending me a fake smile.

"Okay, whatever," I tell her, "I guess we're keeping secrets now, huh?" I ask tilting my head to the side.

She looks at me with panic in her eyes and I know she's feeling conflicted right now.

"It's fine," I tell her, picking up piece of chicken, "Just tell me when you're ready, but I thought we were much closer than that." I say trying to use guilt on her even though I would never pressure her into tell me something she doesn't want to.

"Allison," She whines, "Your making me feel bad, stop it." She tells me sticking out her bottom lip.

"Okay," I say throwing my hands up in surrender, "I'm done, you can keep your little secret."

"Allison!" She says loudly.

"What!"

"You're still making me feel guilty," she tells me with a frown on her face.

"I'm not doing it on purpose," I tell her just as Blake and Will come back to the table.

Instead of Blake sitting next to Jasmine, and Will next to me, they switch seats. Okay, they definitely planned that out while they were gone, so this can't be a good thing.

Blake squeezes in as close to me that he can with a huge smile on his face. Jerk. I know he's doing this crap on purpose just to annoy me. Will glances over at Jasmine nervously and I don't lame him she looks like she's ready to kill him.

Whatever secret these two have must be something good.

Hmm, I wonder if Blake knows what's going on, I'll have to ask him later.

Speak of the devil, that bastards hand just moved to my thigh. Trying not to make a scene, again, I don't remove Blake's hand I simply start munching on my chicken.

"So Jasmin-,

"Shut up," Jasmine says cutting Will off before he can barely get his sentence out.

Well damn, someone's pissy.

Blake watches them in amusement while his hand begins to rub back and forward on my thigh.

Will let's out a sigh but he doesn't try to say anything else. "Trouble in Hell, huh?" Blake says sarcastically with a smirk on his face. I'm not sure if the smirk is because he's rubbing my leg; or just finding them funny.

Jasmine flips him off and I can't help but chuckle. When I do, Blake's hand begins to wonder even more upwards.

Oh goodness.

I look around a bit panicked trying to see if anyone sees his hand. When I look over to see a child at the booth next to ours with wide eyes, I know he sees Blake's hand.

Casually I slide Blake's hand back down towards my knee, away from any private areas. The reason I don't push it all the way off is because I know that he'll just put it back. Plus, I'm pretty sure that he's trying to test me.

"Someone's pissed," He says with a smile on his face looking at Jasmine, knowing he's pissing her off.

"Move," Jasmine says to Will giving him a shove so she can get out of the booth.

Wow, Jasmine is never this grouchy. I wonder what's wrong with her, she's usually happy.

Will stands up out of the booth but he follows Jasmine to wherever she's going leaving me and Blake along.

Shit.

From the corner of my eye I see Blake smirk before he turns to me once gain moving his hand up.

"What?" I ask him narrowing my eyes.

He glances down at his hand on my leg, "Oh nothing," He turns back to his food using his left hand to eat since his right one is on my knee.

This is the moment that our waitress comes to refill our drinks, and flirt with Blake. "Anything I can get you?" She asks but she's speaking to Blake and not me.

Come on now, we're eating the buffet, of course there's nothing she can get him. The only thing she can get him is a drink. It would e a different story if we were eating off the menu that they have.

"Does it have to be on the menu?" Blake asks shooting her a smirk that makes her cheeks turn red.

Oh goodness, is he serious, damn man whore.

"It depends on what you want." She says flipping her hair and licking her Los trying to look sexy but she looks stupid.

I roll my eyes and go back to my food but when I feel Blake's hand slide up even further than before I almost choke on my food

The waitress and Blake both look at me but with different looks on their faces. Blake looks amused and is obviously trying to hold in his laughter. The waitress looks pissed that I interrupted her obvious horrible attempt at flirting.

"What's wrong Allison?" Blake asks innocently before glancing over at the waitress and whispering, "She sometimes have these spasm attacks, it's from her not being right I'm the head." He says tapping my head to make his point.

That whore, did not just say that.

"You know Blake has STDs, right?" I whisper to the waiter in the same tone as Blake before sending him a glare as his mouth drops open.

The waitress has a panicked look on her face, "Uh, I'll go check on some other tables since you two don't need anything." She says and quickly leaves our table.

"You Asswhole," I say shoving Blake as soon as the girl leaves.

"So you're kinky now?" He asks in amusement lifting a brow with a huge smirk on his face.

I choose to ignore that smirk so I won't slap him, "What the hell was that?" I ask him gesturing to my thigh where his hand once was.

"Hey, you weren't complaining," He says with a shrug of his shoulders.

I'm pretty sure my face is red from anger and embarrassment. "I was trying not to cause a scene." I tell him loudly before lowering my lice hen I see people glancing at us, "See," I tell him gesturing to the people watching us.

"Fuck off," Blake says to a guy who's staring a us and the guy instantly looks away.

I slap Blake's shoulder, "That was mean."

He simply waves his hand in annoyance. " You know-" He cuts his sentence off when his phone rings. He glances at the caller ID and lets out a groan on frustration. I try to look and see who's the person but he pulls his phone back, "I gotta take this." He tells me running a hand through his head e for leaving the table without another word.

He did not just seriously ditch me because of a phone call. You've got to be kidding me.

Will comes back to the table without Jasmine with a half smile on his face. I also notice a red hand mark.

"Did Jaz slap you?" I ask in shock.

He shrugs his shoulders, "Eh, I guess I deserved it since I called her a two timing whore." He tells me as he picks up his phone from off our table.

"You called her that and you're still alive?" I ask in shock.

He lets out a chuckle,"Barely, the girl tried to claw my eyes out like Bloody Mary." He tells me.

I simply shake my head knowing Jasmine does stuff like that.

"We're going to head out," He tells me pocketing his phone.

"She's letting you drive her home?" I ask him with wide eyes.

"Yea, but if y'all don't hear from me by morning, assume I'm dead, and Jasmine is my killer." He says patting my head and I slap his hand, "Bye Allison." He tells me before leaving.

So now I'm definitely alone. I wait patiently for Blake to come back to the table even though I know that he's going to irritate me, but that's better than being alone.

Finally Blake comes back to the table with a worried look on his face. "Hey, I've got somewhere to go, Will's going to have to take you home." He tells me sounding apologetic for once.

"Will's already gone." I inform him.

"Are you serious," He asks in frustration and I nod, "Shit," He looks at me for a second and lets out a sigh, "Well it looks like I'm going to have to bring you with me." He says it as if its a punishment.

Wow.

"Well, I didn't realize taking me somewhere Is a punishment." I tell him crossing my arms over my chest in anger.

His eyes widen in shock for a second, "No, I don't mean it like that," he explains, " I'd just rather not take you where I'm going," he runs a hand through his hair in frustration messing it up, "Just come on." He says pulling me out the booth forcefully but gently.

He glances at the table, "Will didn't leave his half, did he?" He asks me.

Now that I think about it he did just leave without leaving money.

"Nope," I say and be shakes his head before getting his alley out. Without paying attention he throws what looks like four twenty bills on the table and drags me towards the exit.

I'm pretty sure our food didn't cost eighty dollars, even adding a tip. Is does he just have this money to blow. I've noticed that everywhere we go together he pulls out money like it grows on trees. I mean he has like stacks and rolls on him.

I'm broken out of my thoughts when the cold air of the night hits my skin. I want to wrap my arms around me but Blake is still tugging on my wrist.

With a sigh I simply follow him to he car but when we get in its cold in the car too. Blake starts up the car and speeds out if the parking lot like cops are after him. He glances over at me and sees that I'm practically shaking so he turns on the heat.

"There's a jacket in the backseat." He tells me keeping his eyes on the road as he makes sharp turns.

"Okay, thanks," I tell him looking behind me in the back seat seeing a black leather jacket. My attention drifts from that when I see what I'm pretty sure is drugs on the floor.

Chapter 17

"Blake, what is this?" I ask picking up the small clear package containing green specimens off the floor. I'm pretty sure that its weed, but I need for him go confirm it.

"What's what?" Blake asks not taking his eyes off the road.

I lean back into my seat taking a deep breath before flashing the package for him to see. He glances at it, "I'm pretty sure you know what it is SweetCheeks." He says picking it from my hands and sticking it in the glove department.

So he's just going to act casual about this, as if there isn't illegal substances in the car.

"Blake, why is that in the car?" I ask him.

"Why are you asking so many questions?" He counters not even glancing at me. He makes a sharp turn and we pull up to what looks like a warehouse.

"Blake, I'm not joking." I tell him crossing my arms over my chest in annoyance.

"I'm not joking either," he says stopping the car.

I narrow my eyes at him, "If you don't answer me, I'll get out of the car and start walking."

He looks at me in amusement with that smirk on his face, "Go for it, your house is back that way." He points in the direction we just came from, "That's about twenty miles, not too bad, since you play soccer, huh?"

I let out a sigh of defeat knowing that I'll either get raped (since its dark outside) or lost. Blake already knew what I would choose, I don't even know why I suggested leaving.

He opens his car door, "I'm guessing that you're staying, so stay in the car I'll be back." He tells me closing is door and locking it with the handset on the keys.

I sit back in my seat still pouting. I don't even know where in the hell we are. All I know is that it's creepy out here. There's a couple of cars and motorcycles on the other side of the lot. The warehouse looks kind of neat surprisingly considering that In movies they're usually run down and beat up.

A knock on my window scares me and breaks me out of my thoughts. I turn to see a cute guy at the window smiling. He has hazel eyes and light brown hair, along with a strong jawline. I'd say that he's around 19.

No matter how cute he is though, I'm not opening this door. He could be one of those cute weirdos who looks for people to abduct and keep hostage just to get off.

"Hello," he says in an accent that I can't quite pick up on. It's hot though.

I pull my eyebrows together in frustration, "Uh hi," I say to him since it seems pretty safe because he can't get to me while I'm in the car.

He sends me a warm smile, "Why don't you get out of the car, it's dark, and it's not too safe out here." He says.

"The only unsafe thing that I see out here is you." I tell him with a frown forming on my face. This is only makes him smirk.

"Well SweetHeart, there are more dangerous things than me out here." He says, "But then again Blake's little groupies always listen to him, and I'm guessing he told you to stay in the car." He says with a smile slowly forming on his face.

Groupie?

Oh hell no. I'm not anyone's groupie, especially Blake's. if I stay in the car it'll look like I'm listening to him which is crazy; Blake doesn't tell me what to do. If I get out of the car I could be kidnapped, then again this guy doesn't look to creepy and he's hot.

Knowing its a poor decision, especially because of my reason, I get out of the car.

The guy smirks, "So one of Blake's groupies defies him, how hot." He says making a blush appear on my face as I close the car door.

I look at him with a glare, "First off I'm not Blake's groupie, and second off I'm hot without defying him." I tell him flipping my hair over my shoulder before turning on my heels and walking in the direction of the warehouse even though I'm not sure where I'm going.

I hear the guy start to walk behind me, "You sure are right about the second one," he says and soon he's walking beside me, "So what's your name?" He asks.

I look up at him debating on wether or not to tell him my name. Really, what could it hurt, I'm already walking in the dark with him, "Allison." I finally tell him as he opens a door and gestures for me to walk in.

"Allison," he repeats and with his accent it sounds different, as crazy as it sounds, that tone was definately hot.

Goodness, what's wrong with me?

I'm walking in the dark with a stranger, and I think him saying my name sounds hot. Maybe I hit my head earlier during the game but I just wasn't aware.

We walk into the room together which has a lot of light. There's people sitting on couches laughing, and smoking. "I'm Zach," he says and I finally recognize his accent.

It's southern.

How could I have missed that?

The people in the room turn their attention to us. Some of them greet Zach while others look at me in curiosity.

"This is Allison." Zach tells them and some mutter a greeting while the others go back to their conversation.

Zach leads me over to a couch that's vacant and gestures for me to sit. I hesitate for a second, but there's no way out now so I go ahead and take a seat. For a second there's an awkward silence before I decide to speak since there's something bugging me.

"Where are you from?" I ask him since that accent has to be from somewhere down south.

He gives me a faint smile, "The most asked question," he tells me, "I'm actually from here, but my mother is from the south so I picked up on her accent as I grew up." He informs me. "How do you know Blake?" He asks curiously raising a brow.

I let out a sigh, "Well you see, we go to school together, and I kind of hit his car, it's kind of a long story." I end up saying.

He smirks, "Well as far as I can tell, we don't have limited time." He tells me propping his feet up on the table in front of the couch and relaxing with his hands behind his head.

Letting out a sigh I start explaining to him my first day of school when I hit Blake. By the end of the story I'm relaxed with my feet on the couch while Zach watches me. We end up moving onto more topics and I learn some things about him; like how he's actually a freshman in college.

"Allison, what are you doing?" I hear someone ask just as a firm grip is placed on my shoulder. I know the voice belongs to Blake but its kind of weird since he called me "Allison" and not one of his crazy nicknames.

I turn to see Blake glaring at Zach and I sigh. So he's going to be an ass again when he's the one who left me in the car alone. I'm pretty sure it's been an hour since me and Zach came inside. Just imagine if I would've still been sitting outside.

Zach smirks at Blake, "Hey Blake, haven't seen you in a while." He says sitting up on the couch.

"Yea whatever," Blake says rudely before redirecting his attention to me, "Lets go," he says pulling me off of the couch. I've never seen him be this pushy and demanding but if he keeps it up I'm going to blow.

Blake starts dragging me out of the building before I can even tell Zach 'bye'. "Why are you being such an ass?" I ask Blake when we're finally both in the car and he's speeding off from the warehouse.

He snaps his head in my direction glaring at me, "Why are you being such a whore? One moment you're flirting and going out with Daniel, now you're flirting with Zach." He shoots back before realization crosses his face.

Guess he didn't mean to say that one out loud.

Well it's said now.

Rage courses through me and before I can think I punch Blake in the face. How he still manages to drive straight on the road with how hard I hit him, I'll never know, but he does it. He didn't even flinch and I can see that the spot Is already red.

"Don't you ever call me a whore again." I tell him in anger wanting to hit him again. "Know what, just don't ever speak to me again." I conclude.

Maybe I'm over reacting but he called me a whore and that hurts. It's not like I'm fooling around with the whole football team. I'm in no kind of committed relationship so I don't see why I can't flirt with who I want. I wasn't even flirting with Zach, we were just talking.

When we pull up to my house, I quickly gather my things and get out of the car slamming the door.

"Allison!" I hear Blake call out from behind me but I don't bother turning around.

Opening my door with my key I go in and close the door shut, locking it behind me. I throw my bags down going into the kitchen to get me something to drink hoping that'll cool me off some. I can tell the house is empty since its quiet and my suspicions are confirmed when I find a note in the kitchen from my mom reading:

Allison,

I've gone out with Beatrice. There's food in the fridge. I'll be back by the time you wake up.

-Mom

I let out a sigh before discarding the note. Beatrice and my mom are like those old women who try to act young; they're always going out. They're also always gambling and losing money. Hell, I'm surprised my mom still has money to pay the rent with.

Grabbing some fruit juice out of the fridge I drink from the bottle not bothering to pour myself a glass. Once I've gotten enough I pull out my phone to call Jasmine.

Maybe she can cheer me up.

The phone rings a couple of times as I head upstairs to my room turning on every light in the house; I won't be like those dumb people on TV.

"Hello," A deep voice says just as I reach my room. The phone was ringing so long I was just about to hang up.

Hmm, who is this?

Maybe it's another one of Jasmine's admirers though I'm sure her mom wouldn't let them in the house at this time of night.

"Hello." The voice says again breaking me out of my thoughts.

"Uh, hello," I say in an unsure tone, "Where's Jaz?"

"Hold on," the voice says and they sound kind of familiar. I hear covers being ruffled before the guy starts talking to someone in the background, "Hey Jasmine get your ass up, somebody's on the phone."

I'm guessing she's sleep.

What time is it anyway?

I glance at the clock on my cable box to see that it's a little passed twelve o'clock, and I sigh.

Did I seriously stay out with Blake that damn long?

"You answered my phone?" I hear Jasmine ask in an angry tone.

"The fucker wouldn't stop ringing," the boy says with a groan.

"Whatever," there's more cover ruffling before Jasmine is finally on the phone, "Hello." She says and by her voice I can tell she was asleep.

"I'm sorry, I didn't mean to wake you." I tell her as I run a hand through my hair before turning the TV on.

"No, it's fine," she says, "What's up?"

Relaxing on my bed I let out a sigh, "I just needed to talk to you but I didn't realize it was this late. Maybe we can talk late-"

"Say no more," She says cutting me off, "We can skip tomorrow and just go to gran's house." She informs me.

A smile comes onto my face as I think about Jasmine's grandma. The woman is hilarious and so laid back you can't help but love her. Whenever Jasmine and I skip school we just go to her house.

"Okay," I agree, "I'll tell you everything tomorrow, and let you go back to sleep." I say still feeling kind of bad for waking her up.

"Alright, bye Alli." And with that she hangs up the phone.

With another sigh I start watching Tv before something dawns on me.

That male voice.

I knew it was recognizable for a reason.

Well I'll be dammed.

That voice belonged to Will.

Chapter 18

"Hey, wake your ass up!" Someone says tugging on my clothes. With a sigh I bury my head deeper into my pillow and ignore the person.

"Allison, get up dammit," the person starts to basically pound their fist on the back of my legs. I let out a grunt before rolling over to see Jasmine standing above me with Will behind her.

What's he doing here?

I know Jasmine's suppose to be taking me to her grandma's house, but where did Will come from?

Jasmine sighs, "When he found out that we're skipping he wouldn't stop bothering me until I agreed to let him come with us." She informs me probably picking up on the look on my face.

"And how did he know that we're skipping?" I ask her skeptically sitting up in my bed as I remember Will answering her phone last night.

Jasmine glances back at Will while a mischievous smirk makes its way onto his face. When Jasmine turns around to face me there's a glare on her face.

Ha, she's caught now.

"Get dressed and lets go." She says completely ignoring my question before pushing Will out of the room and following behind him.

Shaking my head I get out of bed to get ready but thoughts of Jasmine and Will still run through my head.

What's up with those two?

One minute they're sort of getting along. The next minute they're arguing and Jasmine slaps him. Hell, Will had to be at her house last night, in her bed. It was late I heard covers moving when he gave the phone to her. She was pissed he answered her phone. There's a bunch of janky shit going on there. I'll have to ask her about it later.

When I'm finally dressed in a pair of shorts and a tank top I head downstairs. In all honesty the only people I'm expecting to be downstairs is Jasmine and Will. Blake being downstairs too is a huge surprise. Memories of him calling me a whore flashes through my mind. I know this Asswhole must be out of his mind if he thinks I'm okay with him being here too.

"What's he doing here?" I ask Jasmine looking in her direction.

She shrugs her shoulders oblivious to the fact that Blake and I aren't on speaking terms, "He told him about us skipping." She says pointing at Will.

It's only now that I notice Will is basically invading my refrigerator. When he feels everyone's gaze on him he turns around with a piece of cheese hanging out of his mouth.

Is he serious?

"You are not seriously eating cheese by itself." Jasmine says turning her nose up at him.

He shoots her a smile with a shrug if his shoulders before continuing to go through my fridge.

I simply roll my eyes and decide to leave him alone. "Can we just go?" I ask still pissed off.

The point of today was for me and Jasmine to finally get some actual girl talk in. We haven't been able to do it in a while and there's some things we really need to cover. Blake and Will being the top things on that list.

"Yeap," Jasmine says walking over to the fridge and grabbing Will by his shirt. "Lets go." She tells him hauling him out of the fridge.

He lets out a grunt but lets her pull him towards the kitchen's door. We all walk out of the house and the only cars outside belong to Will and Blake.

"We can take Will's car and I'm driving,"Jasmine declares before anyone can even ask about the seating arrangement. She snatches Will 's keys out of his pocket and heads over to his polished red pickup truck.

He glares at Jasmine but lets her take the keys. I hurry to the car and sit in the passenger seat so I won't have to be stuck in the back with Blake.

"Hey no fair, it's my car, how come I can't ride shotgun?" Will complains frowning at me.

Jasmine glares at him as she cranks up his car, "Hey, shut up and get in the car, or I'll leave you." She tells him and I'm pretty sure the threat isn't hollow.

With a pout Will slides into the back next to Blake who's already in the truck.

By the time we make it to Jasmine's grandma's house I'm pretty sure Will is on the verge of having a heart attack.

"Jasmine what were you thinking?" He exclaims as we get out of the car and Jasmine simply smiles at him.

"I don't know what you're talking about," She tells him slipping his keys into her back pocket.

"I'm pretty sure you almost ran my poor baby ink a thousand things," he says shaking his head, "Plus, you ran at least ten red lights, and four stop signs, I'm going to be mailed a ticket for at least six of those violations." He complains.

She pats her head which she basically has to stand on her tippy toes to do, "Oh stop stressing, it'll be fine." With those last words to him she turns on her Hell's and we head to her grandma's porch.

Jasmine's grandma -Londie- has a pretty big house. It's not mansion size but its something to gawk at. At the age of sixty the woman gets around like a teenager and she's always making money doing something, whether its decorating for someone's wedding or cleaning up a house. Her house is a big brown two story with a porch that faces the streets where you'll usually find her. I'm actually surprised she isn't out here today.

Jasmine doesn't bother knocking on the door she simply pulls out her key to the house and unlocks the door. Blake and Will follow us into the house as Will fidgets with the hem of his shirt.

"Grandma!" Jasmine calls out as we pass the living room and make our way into the dinning room.

I hear footsteps on the stairs before Londie appears with a pair of gloves on, she smiles when she sees us. "What are y'all doing here?" She asks giving us both a hug.

"Didn't feel like going to school," Jasmine tells her and Londie nods as if she understands.

"Who's this?" She asks looking in the direction of the boys who're being awfully quiet.

"This is Will," she says gesturing to him, "and that's Blake." She points at him.

"Well I'm Londie, but just call me whatever you want." She tells them with a smile giving them both a hug which I'm sure surprises them.

"Where's grandpa?" Jasmine asks her.

Londie rolls her eyes, "That man's outside doing something." She says with a wave of her hand, "I was in the basement cleaning so I have no idea what he's doing." She says.

"Okay," Jasmine tells her and we head out back to find her grandpa.

Mr. Jeffrey is a really nice man I'd I say so myself. He's always spoiling Jasmine and I, and he's very friendly.

We find him pulling up weeds from the ground. The lawn mower and hedge cutter are out to so I'm pretty sure he's just doing yard work.

"Well look who dropped in," He says when he sees us as he wipes sweat from his face with the back of his hand.

"Hey Grandpa," Jasmine says giving him a hug.

He gives me a hug to before Jasmine introduces the guys. "You know grandpa, if you want they can help you with the yard." She says volunteering the boys to help.

"Nah it's okay," he says.

"No, I insist," she says giving the, both a shove towards the yard supplies.

Mr. Jeffrey looks hesitant for a second, "Well okay," he says before starting to tell them what to do.

Jasmine and I leave the boys outside and go back in the house. Jasmine snags a bottle of wine from the kitchen and we go upstairs to the room that basically belongs to her.

She closes the door behind us before turning on the TV as we sit on the couch in the room. She pops open the top on the wine before looking at me.

"Sorry about the boys, once Will found out he wouldn't stop bugging me about coming, so I finally gave in." She informs me.

"It's okay," I say with a sigh relaxing on the couch.

"So what did you want to talk about?" She asks after taking a swig of the wine and passing the bottle to me.

"Where do you want to start?" I take a sip of the wine happy that its sweet and not bitter, "There's Blake, school, you and Will." I turn my eyes in the direction of her and she looks guilty.

She scratches the back of her neck and tries not to make eye contact. Finally she lets out a sigh and looks at me, "What's up with you and Blake?" She asks tilting her changing the subject.

I glare at her but I don't say anything else about Will, "He's an ass." I tell her with a frown on my face.

"Explain more," She says.

By the time Jasmine and I have finished half the bottle of wine, and discussed what happened with Blake, Will comes upstairs.

"Hey babe," Will says when he comes in the room and I'm in shock. Will scratches the back of his neck as he realize what he said, "Uh grandma said for you two to come down and eat." With those words he hurriedly leaves the room.

I raise an eyebrow at Jasmine who lets out a grunt and stands up from the couch. "So babe-" she glares at me before I can finish my sentence and I laugh.

It's so obvious something is going on between them.

We head downstairs to find Blake and Will sitting at the table in the dinning room. They're both sweaty from working outside but there's what look like glasses of kool aid.

Blake and Will are both looking at the glasses skeptically and I can't help but chuckle.

"Uh, it's kool aid," Jasmine says rolling her eyes at them no sitting down at the table next to Blake obviously trying to stay away from Will. They both look clueless still, "Dude, you guys totally fit white people stereotype when it comes to kool aid." Jasmine says chuckling and I know she's not being racist. I take the empty seat next to Will.

Londie comes in with a tray that has four plates on it with burgers and onion rings. Two of the burgers are already fixed while the other two have toppings on the side.

"I know how Allison, and Jasmine eat their burgers, I wasn't too sure about you two so I just put it on the side." She informs them.

"Thank you," they both say before she leaves us to eat.

It's silent around the table and I'm pretty sure it's for a lot of reasons. One being Blake and I aren't talking, it's actually weird that we haven't talked all day. Another reason being Will's slip up of calling Jasmine 'babe'.

"Grandma!" Will suddenly yells breaking the silence causing everyone to jump.

Londie rushes into the dinning room with a worried look on her face as we all stare at Will. "What's wrong?" She asks him.

"Can I have another burger, this is amazing." He tells her causing everyone to glare at him.

He did not just holler like a crazy person because he wants another burger.

Londie looks shocked but she can't help but let a smile come onto her face, "Okay sweetie, there's some extra ones in the kitchen, I'll go get you one." She tells him before going in the kitchen.

"Dumbass," Jasmine mutters but instead of being offended Will smiles, which is probably because he's happy Jasmine actually spoke to him.

Londie comes back to the dining room and gives Will the burger. He eagerly starts to pile stuff onto the burger. She also sets two wine glasses in front of Jasmien and I.

"What's this for?" I ask her.

She smiles faintly at us, "If you're going to drink, do it from a glass, it's much more classier." She says and I'm not surprised she knows that we took one of the whine bottles.

She turns to Will, "And you son, I like you, so next time you come over, make sure you don't have the munchies." She tells him.

"How did you-"

"Son, I know the signs, and you've been eating every since you got here." She tells him, "You were even eating while trying to cut the grass."

Blake lets out a chuckle and she turns her attention to him, "Hey, I could smell the weed coming off of you so now laughing." She tells him pointing a finger at him.

How did this woman notice all of this when I didn't.

She shoots us a smile before leaving again.

"Damn she's good." Will says taking another huge bite of his burger.

After we eat we all go back to Jasmine's room and watch TV. Jasmine and I both sit on the bed while the boys sit on the couch. Will and Jasmine rage about what to watch, but Jasmine wins as usual so we end up watching "The Cleveland Show"

'My name is Cleveland Brown,

And I am proud to be...'

As the theme song for the fifth episode comes on I stand up to go to the bathroom. After I'm done I come back to the room to find Will sitting in my spot next to Jasmine. I glare at him before reluctantly taking a seat next to Blake on the couch. I sit as far away from him as I can and put my feet in between us. Jasmine shoots me a glare and I roll my eyes.

Earlier when I told Jasmine about what happened with Will she told me I didn't react right. She informed me that I should've have punched the taste out of his mouth and made him beg for my forgiveness. She also said that I should start trying to make him win me over. It really doesn't surprise me at all that she basically wants for me to get revenge on him.

"Jasmine, honey, I need to talk to you." Londie says sticking her head in the room and Jasmine leaves to see what she wants.

There's an awkward silence in the room which is basically M and Blake's fault. Will glances at us before saying, "Awkward." he then goes back to watching Tv.

Jasmine comes back into the room with a huge smile on her face. "What?" I ask her as she sits down next to Will.

"The 'G' parents are going out of town." She says happily and I already know why she's excited.

"Why are you happy about that?" Blake asks finally speaking since we got here today.

"Because I'm there favorite grandchild, so they always leave Allison and I to watch over there house. They also purposely leave out all their alcohol out." She tells Blake and Will.

"They leave us with a good four hundred dollars too." I add in.

"Basically everything to throw a party." Jasmine says and the boys finally catch on.

"I think we should charge five dollars a head." Jasmine says and I nod my head in agreement.

"You charge a fee to get in the party" Will asks in shock.

"Hell yea we charge a fee you dumbass so be prepared to pay up." She tells him. "Hey I'm going to need for you to let me borrow your truck." She says as a thoughtful look crosses her face.

"Why?" Will whines.

"Because I need to go get snacks, if it makes you happy you can come with me." She tells him and he perks up.

Wait if they go together that means I have to stay with Blake.

Alone.

Chapter 19

It's the only thing in the room while Blake and I don't talk. Neither of us have even bothered to change the TV so it's on the Cleveland show. In all honesty if someone where to tell me a couple of days ago that Blake and I could sit in a room without him making passes at me or arguing I would call them crazy.

For about thirty minutes Jasmine and Will argued about when to throw the party before they decided to throw two; one tonight and one Friday. Obviously since we have the money to throw two there was no complaints. They left to drop Londie and Mr.Jeffery off at the train station and to go to the store.

The drive to the train station should be about an hour. Knowing Will and Jasmine they'll take a good two hours in the store; 75% of that will be used arguing.

So Blake and I will be alone approximately three hours, take and give some minutes.

A phone ringing interrupts the awkward silence in the room. I check my pockets hoping its mine before realizing its actually Blake's phone. With a sigh he sticks his hand into his pocket before pulling out his phone.

He looks at the caller ID before letting out a frustrated groan, "What?" He answers in a not so nice way.

"No, why would I let you do that." He listens to the person on the phone while I study his facial expression, finally with a sigh he looks directly at me for the first time today, "Here," he says passing me the phone easily since we're both sitting on the couch.

With a frown I accept the phone wondering who it is, "Hello," I say in an unsure tone.

"Allison," The southern drawl comes from the other end of the phone and I know who it is.

"Oh hey Zach," I say sitting up straighter on the couch. I hear Blake let out a groan before he changes whats on TV.

"Hey, what are you doing today?" He asks me casually.

I rub the back of my neck, "A party," I tell him, "Interested in coming?" I ask him and I feel Blake's glare burning a whole in the side of my face.

I shirt again and accidentally hit the speaker button, "Sure," he answers in a quite happy tone that echoes through the room "But what are you doing right now?" He questions as I'm about to hit the speaker button to turn it off.

In a second the phone is snatched from my grasp, "Sorry Zach, but she's kind of busy right now." Blake says into the phone turning the speaker off. "It's my phone so no, now goodbye." He hangs up the phone before sticking it back in his pocket.

I can't help but stare at him in shock. He looks at me with annoyance written clear across his face. "What?" He asks in a bitter tone.

"Was it really necessary to be that rude?" I ask him narrowing my eyes.

"Like I said it's my fucking phone, I have the right to decide who talks to who on it, and by frankly I don't want you talking to Zach." He tells crossing his arms over his chest trying to show that he's in charge.

Like hell he is.

I jump off of the couch in anger, "You know what I think you become even more of an ass everyday!" I shout at him, "Just when we were starting to tolerate each other you just had to mess everything up by being an ass!"

Blake visibly grinds his teeth trying to calm his anger but I'm not done with him.

"I was just talking to a guy and you called me a whore, it's not like we're nothing besides acquaintances, we're not even really fried s so I don't see what gives you the right to act like a jealous boyfriend."

I can tell that I've pissed Blake off when he stands up from the couch himself, "That's what this is about, you're still pissed about last night, get over it Allison!"

There's a lot of things wrong with the sentence Blake just said.

One; He called me Allison, not Sweetcheeks, Bambi, or any of his other ridiculous nicknames.

Two; He thought I was over what happened last night.

And three; He wants me to drop what happened last night.

"You expect me to fucking forgive you when you basically called me a hoe " I yell as my last bit of patience left me.

"Well when your prancing around flirting with everything that has a cock and leading them on, what you expect me to call you!"

You know how I wanted to slap Blake last night well I'm feeling that again. Of course I don't slap him though.

Nope.

I simply punch the shit out of him.

Blake doesn't flinch one bit from my punch but there's a bruise already forming. I'm still pissed though. "Who do I lead on?" I shout at him as I reel my hand back to punch him again.

Just as I swing Blake grabs my wrist and grips it pretty hard. "Everyone," he says in an angry whisper.

I take a deep breath before looking him in the eyes, "And who is everyone?" I ask harshly.

He pulls me close to him by my wrist with a dead lock grip, "You really don't want me to answer that question." He says.

"And why don't I?" I question him pulling back a little so I can look at his face more. His jaw is locked tight while his eyes are cold.

He leans down close to my ear and I'm no longer able to study his features. Heat runs through my body and I can feel his breath on my neck. "Because some stuff should be left unsaid unless you really want to create a problem."

"What kind of problems are you referring to?" I ask him letting curiosity get the best of me.

Before I can react Blake moves away from my ear and pulls me fully against him. He plants his soft lips firmly against mine, and I slowly feel myself giving into him.

I know just a second ago I punched him and he called me a hoe, but I just can't pull away.

Blake's hand runs up and down along my back as my hands entangle in his hair. He backs me up into the wall gently and I wrap my legs around his waist.

Tingles go through my body and I seriously just want to melt.

Once again Blake changes our position as he holds me firmly and lays me on the bed. My legs are still around his waist and my back's on the bed. Blake basically pries my lips open and slips his tongue into my mouth.

Not again.

I really want to kill someone right now.

Blake pulls away from my lips but stays firmly where he is. We both look to the door to find Will and Jasmine staring at us.

Dammit.

Slowly Blake moves away from me as I sit up on the bed, and there's silence. It's like everyone is just staring at each other as if we can magically make this awkwardness disappear.

"I have to seriously sanitize my bed now." Jasmine says breaking the silence.

"What are you two doing here?" Blake asks in annoyance running a hand through his hair.

Will has a smirk on his face, "Sorry about the clock block bro, but I forgot my wallet." He says gesturing to the nightstand where his Wallet sitting on the nightstand.

Jasmine has a look of disgust on her face as she looks at her bed, "I'm going to need some fabuloso." She turns to look at me, "You two are coming with us." She says, "I'm all for y'all hooking up, heck I've been encouraging it since day one, but not in my bed." She says shaking her head before turning on her heels and heading out the door.

With a sigh of embarrassment I follow after her leaving the boys in the room.

"Hey, we'll meet back up with y'all." Jasmine tells the boys when we're inside the store, "We have to make a stop at the cleaning supplies." She grabs a buggy as we part ways with the boys.

I follow her to the aisle contains cleaning supplies, "I'm so disappointed in you," she says shaking her head, "When you decide to take a dip into the hot pool that is Blake, you decide to do it in my bed at my grandma's house." She picks up a bottle of blue liquid cleanser.

"We're going to need stuff to clean up its after the party too." She throws a box of garbage bags into the buggy along with some other things.

"Okay we're good here," she declares, as we head to the snack aisle.

"Your so quiet," she says glancing back at me before throwing bags of chips in the buggy, "Who's Zach?" She asks randomly.

I raise a brow, "Why?" I ask her.

"He called Will's phone claiming that he was invited to the party by you but he wasn't given the address, something about Blake hanging the phone up." She explains before examining some dips, after a thought she gets them all.

I shrug when she looks at me, "Just a new friend, if I can even call him that, every time I talk to him Blake throws a bitch." I tell her picking up a bag of takis and throwing them in the buggy.

"Is he hot?" Jasmine asks.

I glance at her, "Of course he is," I tell her.

She clucks her tongue, "Well you see that's the problem Blake's just jealous."

I frown at her, "Why would Blake be jealous?" I ask her.

She gives me a look of annoyance, "You're just so damn oblivious the guy always has a look in his eye when he's looking at you." She explains.

"What kind of look?" I ask her hating that she's being so vague.

"Well.." She says drawing the word out, "There's that one look that definatelty means he wants to fuck you."

My eyes widen as I glare at her. The grandma who's on the aisle with us has a look of disgust on her face before moving onto another aisle.

"Then there's that look he has and I can tell he just wants to hold you and all that other gushy stuff." We move onto another aisle, "Heck I wouldn't be surprised if he confessed his undying love for you." She chuckles at the thought.

"You're reading into stuff wrong," I tell her rolling my eyes.

"Whatever, can I have that Zach guy then since Blake is obviously not going to let you have him."

I just shake my head at her, "What about you and Will?" I ask hoping she'll finally tell me what's going on.

I hate not knowing stuff.

She snorts, "What about us?"

"There's obviously something going on in between y'all." I tell her.

"You're wrong." She tells me.

"I think not," I argue, "Boo, I know you like the back of my hand, I also know who was in your bed last night."

She turns around sharply and I smirk at her with my arms across my chest.

Ha, she's caught now.

"It's not even like that," she says with a sigh.

"Oh, then what is it like?" I question her tilting my head to the side.

She shrugs just as Blake and Will come around the corner with a buggy full of food, and alcohol. I even see brownie mix in the mix of all the junk they have.

"I love fake IDs," Will says pulling his out if his pocket. It looks just like a real one so if I didn't know it was fake I would think it's real.

Jasmine peeps in at his ID, "Oh man yours is better than mine," she pulls out hers and they discuss things that old give away the fake ness.

I simply shake my head at them before glancing at Blake. He looks as if he's in his own world. There's a deep concentrated look on his face as he stares off into space. He finally turns and looks at me before glancing away.

So we're back to acting awkward.

"Allison have a drink!" Jasmine basically yells at me over the music.

It's around nine o'clock and our party started a little over thirty minutes ago. I'm not quite sure who invited them all but there's at least already one hundred people here.

Hell, I've never even seen half these people a day in my life so I'm sure they don't even go to our school.

I squint my eyes at Jasmine; someone had the great idea of turning off the lights and just having those weird flashy ones on, so it's pretty hard to see.

"Thanks," I yell back accepting the drink from her as she watches me with curious eyes, there's as mischievous glint in them.

"No problem," she says with a grin as I take a huge gulp of the drink.

Once I'm done with the drink I see. That her grin grows even wider, "What's your problem?" I ask tilting my head at her.

"Oh nothing," she says tilting her head got the side with a smirk.

"What are you up to?" I call out but she's already blending in with the crowd so I can't see her.

I let out a sigh before making my way to the kitchen to grab something to eat. There's a variety of foods but the brownies catch my eye the most. Will and Jasmine baked them earlier while I set everything up.

I eat one and I swear it tastes like heaven in my mouth.

When I'm on my sixth brownie I feel a presence beside me "Mind if I have one?" A familiar voice asks and I know exactly who it is.

I turn around with a smile on my face, "Hey Zach," I tell him as he smiles at me. He reaches over me to grab a brownie of his own.

For some reason Zach squints his nose up before sniffing the brownie. He removes it from his nose before smiling at me, "You do know these are hash brownies, right?" He asks me raising a brow as he takes a bite of his brownie.

Hash brownies?

Huh?

Shit.

You've got to be kidding me.

"Are you serious?" I ask him and he nods, "I'm going to kill Will and Jasmine."

"Hey if you're going to kill me do it tomorrow, because I've already got my vibe going." Jasmine says coming into my view with a grin on her face.

She looks at Zach and her grin widens, "Well, hello Sexy." She leans against the counter where the brownies are, she eyes Zach up and down before looking at his face with a smirk.

Okay, Jasmine sober is crazy. Jasmine drunk, and apparently high, is much worse. The girl is always sexual, and drunk it's just crazy. The way she's looking at Zach I know she's going to say something that's just outrageous.

She looks him over once more, and I guess she decides that she likes what she sees because she finally speaks, "If I flip a coin, what are my chances of getting head?"

She did not just say that.

Zach looks shocked for a second but not for too long, "Well I've got a coin in my pocket we could test out your chances."

"Okay, and this is where I leave the room." I tell them sliding between them and heading back into the room that's basically the dance floor.

I make my way into the middle of the people and start dancing. People start to dance with me and I don't even check to see who, I just go along with it. After a while I've had at least six drinks and twenty different dance partners. My head starts to hurt a little and my body is pretty heated. I feel careless and light.

Hands on my waist cause me to turn around but I can't see the person because they instantly plant their lips on mine. I don't push them away even though I'm not sure who it is. I simply kiss them back as our lips move in sync.

We finally pull away and I look up to see Blake. There's something in his eyes that isn't usually there. He also has this soft expression on his face as he looks at me.

We dance together and make out for a while and before I know it we've made our way back to Jasmine's room with the door locked.

Blake kisses me deeply as my hands fumble with his belt. Eventually we're both left in nothing but our undergarments.

I entangle my hands through his hair as he places kisses along my neck.

Blake pulls back and looks into my eyes; searching for something. I guess he finds what he's looking for in my eyes because soon we're in no man's land and there's no turning back.

A loud irritating noise wakes me up and for a second I think it's an alarm befor I realize it's my phone. I sit up letting out a groan as a major headache hits me. There's a throbbing in the back of my head. There's a slight pain in my legs and the worst of all I'm naked in the bed with some guy.

My phone stops ringing and I focus on who's next to me. I can't remember much from last night but I'm pretty sure I know what happened. Pulling back the cover I see Blake's face.

I let out a relieved sigh since I at least didn't hookup with some random guy like the girls in books usually do.

My phone starts ringing again and I quickly answer it so it'll stop ringing.

"What?" I basically yell into the phone.

The person on the other end of the phone lets out a chuckle, "Well, that's no way to talk to your father, now is it?"

Chapter 20

"Hey Dad," I say running a hand through my hair as I look around the room with my eyes trying to locate my clothes.

"Hey Sweetie why are you so grumpy this morning?" He asks casually as if we talk everyday.

Like that would ever happen.

"Oh, just a long night," I tell him as I shuffle out of bed and grab my underwear when I see them thrown on the couch.

I try to hold the phone with my neck and shoulder as I slip on my undergarments.

Now to locate my shirt and shorts.

"Honey, I'm going to send you some money for it."

Huh?

"What dad?" I ask obviously missing what he said a little while ago.

"I want you to come out and visit me, you can bring Jasmine along, I'll send you the money for the tickets." He retells me and I let out a sigh.

Of course he thinks I'll come see him if he lets Jasmine come with me.

"Dad." I say letting out a sigh.

"Bring whoever you want, I'll send six tickets, is that enough?" He asks continuing to try and bribe me.

"Fine dad," I say letting out another sigh.

I really don't want to deal with him right now.

"Okay honey, love you, see you when you get here." My dad says and the line goes dead.

Leave it to him to be short and sweet.

I find my shorts and slip them on but it's impossible to find my damn shirt. With a sigh I sit down on the bed an put my head in my hands.

So many years of fooling around with guys and keeping my virginity intact wasted.

Hell, I can barely even remember most of last night. All I remember is Jasmine passing me drinks as if someone told her alcohol would be discontinued after last night.

I stand up from the bed deciding to just go downstairs with a bra and shorts on. The house is trashed and there's red solo cups everywhere.

I make my way to the kitchen where I find Jasmine and Will arguing, well at least I hear them since I haven't entered yet.

"They're going to be so pissed." Jasmine exclaims a d I can tell she's trying to keep her voice down.

"They'll get over it," Will tells her, "Hell, we don't even have to tell them what we did, it isn't like they weren't already going to jump each others bones."

Why do I have a feeling they're talking about Blake and I?

"True," Jasmine says letting out a sigh.

I walk into the kitchen with a glare on my and they both look shocked. Jasmines' standing by the fridge while Will is drinking water, probably trying to get rid of his hangover.

Now that I think about it I need to be trying to get rid of my headache.

Wait, they're not off the hook.

I continue to glare at them and they both look guilty, "What did you two do?" I ask grabbing a bottle of water out of the fridge.

Will glances at Jasmine and she redirects her attention to the ground.

Definitely Guilty.

"One of you better start speaking." I say just as Blake walks into the kitchen with a frown on his face.

He glances at me for a while before looking away.

I take a long gulp of my water waiting for one of them to confess.

Zach walks into the room and he looks just as trashed as everyone else in the room. Will looks up at him before glancing at Jasmine -who looks guilty- before glaring at Zach.

I'll have to ask about that later.

"Aphrodisiac," I hear Will mutter.

"What?" Blake asks looking at him funny as he snatches my water out of my hand and starts to drink.

Wow, he barely glances at me but steals my water.

What a gentleman.

"He said Aphrodisiac," Jasmine says.

Zach gives them both a strange look, "Like Aphrodite aphrodisiac?" He questions.

"Yea," Will mutters avoiding making eye contact with me or Blake.

I start to put all the pieces together.

"You drugged us!" I say loudly and everyone in the room cringes from their hangovers.

Right now I don't even care about my hangover.

"It was suppose to be a prank," Jasmine says moving close to Will.

"A fucking prank where I screwed this idiot," I say pointing at Blake who frowns at me, "and I can't even remember losing my virginity."

Who pulls a prank like that?

"Well you were sort of high and drunk too so it's not completely our fault." Will says.

My eyes widen and I take a deep breath trying to calm myself.

"I'm just going to act like this never happened." I say through gritted teeth.

Blake brushes past me but not before whispering in my ear though, "You can never forget your first."

Chapter 21

I finally calm down enough to invite Jasmine to come with me to my dad's so I go back to the kitchen to find her. Everyone's sitting at the table while Zach is cooking something. The air is filled with tension. I've no idea what happened last night but I know Will's mad at Jasmine and wants to kick Zach's ass.

Everyone watches me as I take a seat at the table. Will and Jasmine look guilty while Blake looks annoyed.

I glance at Jasmine, "My day's sending me six tickets to come visit him." I tell her and she smiles.

She's not fully forgiven yet.

"Would it make you feel better if I invite four hot guys to come with us?" She asks with a mischievous smile obviously trying to get me to forgive her.

Will and Zach both look at her after the statement she made.

"No, Blake and I are going." Will says volunteering to come with us.

Blake doesn't say anything he just folds his arms over his chest pouting like a child.

"Uh, if they go I get to go too." Zach says pointing at Blake and Will.

"They barely know you." Will spits out at him with a frown on his face.

He has a point...

"They barely know you two."

Know that I come to think about it..

"We've been hanging out for two months." Will argues back.

Well that is true.

Wait.

Two months?

"That evil munchkin." I say out loud and everyone looks at me weirdly.

I ignore them pulling out my phone to call the manipulator.

"Hello," my mother says answering her phone.

"Mom, it's been two months, why isn't my car fixed?" I ask her.

The deal was she'd give me back my car after a month because I watched the kids a couple of times.

"Oh dear," she says and I can hear her laughing.

I also hear Beatrice laughing too.

What's there problem.

"Please don't tell me you're drunk this early in the morning." I say with a groan.

"That's none of your business." She tells me confirming my suspicions, "Speaking of early, why aren't you at school?" She asks me and my eyes grow wide.

"Uh," think of a lie Allison, "I sprung my ankle playing soccer and it hurts to walk." I lie since my mom hasn't seen me since my soccer game, it really shows how great of a mother she is, "So, I'm at Jasmine's grandparents house with her since she stayed home with me."

Ha, whoever said I was a bad liar suck on that.

"Okay sweety," My mom says and I know if she wasn't intoxicated she would be able to tell I'm lying.

"So what about my car mom?" I ask.

"Oh, you can get it when you come back from with your dad." She tells me.

When is that again, I didn't hear him, "And that's when?"

"Friday." She tells me before the line goes dead.

Well she didn't even say "love you" or a simple "bye."

Zach walks into the room setting a plate of eggs and bacon down in front of Jasmine and I.

He barely sits my plate down before I start dodging into it.

He goes back to the kitchen to get his own plate and sits next to Jasmine when he comes back. Blake and Will are both glaring at him, I'm not sure if its from him not fixing them a plate; or because they just don't like him. I'm thinking both.

"Why would your dad send you six tickets, isn't that a bit overboard?" Zach asks choosing to ignore Blake and Will.

"Her day's loaded and always trying to win her over." Jasmine says with mouth full of food.

How lady like.

I wipe my mouth with a napkin, "Yea, my dad owns some company so he has a lot of money." I explain, "That's why I have a camaro, he bought it to try to butter me up."

"Why's he trying to butter you up?" Will asks as he stops glaring at Zach.

"Well you see, pappy dearest apparently had an affair while with my mom; and when I turned six we learned he had a son the same age as me." I explain, "So we've never quite gotten along, he stays in Miami w-"

"Miami!" Will exclaims, "You definitely have to take me with you now." He says, "Do you know how many hot babes live there?"

"Well considering the fact that I never pay attention to hot babes, no." I say rolling my eyes at him.

"I mean really who else are you guys going to take, from what I can tell the girl's at our school don't really like you." He says.

"Yea, but the males love us." I say with a smirk on my face.

"Take us or I'll tell your mom that you lied about your ankle." Blake says finally speaking up.

Well you see my mom likes Blake better than me so there's no doubt she'll believe him, and yell at me.

Shit.

"Stop kicking my seat." I hiss turning around to look at Blake and Will.

We're on the airplane and unfortunately Will and Blake are with us, along with Zach and David. Jasmine and I are sitting together, the idiots are behind us, and Zach and David are sitting In front of us.

"What are you talking about?" Blake asks trying to sound innocent.

So about a day after the party Blake decided to go back to annoying the hell out of me.

"You know what I'm talking about!" I basically yell at him.

Jasmine rolls her eyes from beside me and Will shakes his head.

"How about we trade seats so he can't kick you." Will suggests.

"Fine," I say grabbing my ipad and trading seats with Will.

I stick my earbuds in my ears and turn my back on Blake who's smirking at me.

'You won't find him trying to chase the devil

for money, fame, for power, out of grief'

Poke

'you won't ever find him where the rest go

you will find him, you'll find him next to me'

Poke

'Next to me ooooh'

Poke

'Next to me ooooh'

Poke

'Next to me ooooh'

I yank earbuds out of my ear and turn around to glare at Blake, "If you poke me one more fucking time I'm going to choke you." I threaten him and he smirks.

"Have you always been this violent?" He asks still smirking.

Somebody kill me now.

Our taxi pulls up to the gated house that I've only been to about five times my whole life and I let out a sigh. I'm currently riding Inbetween Zach and Jasmine which is a relief because Blake aggravated me the whole plane ride here.

Zach passes the driver a twenty dollar bill telling him to keep the change before he opens his door and gets out; he waits until Jasmine and I both are out of the car before closing it.

What a gentleman.

Unlike the three getting out of the taxi behind us.

"Damn!" Will says gawking at my dad's mansion and I roll my eyes.

Since he's expecting us dad's gates are already open. David, and Jasmine have already been here with me before so they aren't staring as much as The three who haven't.

I march up the stone steps leading to my dad's mansion before pounding on the door and ringing the doorbell.

I need a nap from dealing with Blake for a good six hours straight.

The door opens and I smile when I see who's standing at the door, "Ace!" I yell wrapping my arms around him and he chuckles.

"Alli, I've missed you too." He says smiling and engulfing me in a hug.

When we pull away from each other he gives Jasmine a hug too, "I haven't seen you in forever shorty." He says ruffling her hair and she smacks his had but there's a smile on her face.

Him and David exchange greetings before he leads us into the house.

"I thought you had moved out of here." I tell Ace sitting down on one of the couches in the living room.

"Well I did but unfortunately I just moved back in about a week ago." He says.

"Who's he?" I hear Blake ask Jasmine.

"You idiot," she says smacking him in the back of the head and he lets out a help, "Can't you tell, he's her brother."

Chapter 22

"You know I've missed you little sis." Ace says ruffling my hair and hugging me again.

"Hey you're barely even older than me." I tell him laughing as I poke him in the chest.

Our mothers had us like a day apart and people usually mistake us for twins since we look so much alike; with our black hair and blue eyes. Needless to say we get most of our looks from our father. I've always had a theory that somehow dad purposely made sure our births were close together. I really wouldn't be surprised. He probably did it so his possibilities of having a son to run his company would be greater.

"If I'm not mistaken, I'm 18 hours older than you."

"It dosen't matter because I'm smarter." I say sticking my tongue out at him.

"I've already scored a 30 on my ACT." He replies very proud of his high score.

I smirk at him, "31." I shoot back telling him my score.

"She's lying." He says looking at Jasmine in disbelief.

They look at each other for a second and I see something pass between both of their eyes.

Oh no.

"I'd be lying if I said she's lying." Jasmine finally answers redirecting her eyes, and Ace turns back to me.

"Holy shit Al."

"Already expecting scholarships from some of the best colleges." I tell him, "Just imagine what I'm going to score as a senior next year."

"I bet you a hundred dollars that I can beat your score." He says sticking his hand out to me and I smirk.

"Deal." I say taking his hand in mine.

When I'm usually around Ace we make bets with large amounts of money because we'll simply get it from dad. To say our dad likes to blow money is an understatement. If the man wasn't so successful he'd be living in a ditch right now from being broke. He's always trying to give my mother money but she rarely ever accepts it. Me on the other hand when he deposits money into my bank account every month I accept it without hesitation. He's the main reason I don't bother with getting a job.

Why work for money when someone can easily give it to you?

"Allison dear, I see you've made it." My father says descending from the stairs leading to the room we're in. His blue eyes flicker to the boys but he doesn't say anything. My father is like an older looking version of Ace, black hair, deep blue eyes, tall, and he's actually still pretty built for his age.

"Jasmine, David, it's nice to see you, it's been a while." My dad says giving them a smile that they return.

He walks over to me and gives me a hug, "I've missed you honey, you really should come and stay with me." He says releasing me from his firm grip.

"I've told you that's not happening." I tell him with a frown.

As if I'm going to leave my mother and friends to come and stay here. Even if the house is amazing, and has personal servants.

"At least come and stay for the summer." He tries to convince me.

"I'll think about it." I say with a sigh and his face brightens before he turns to the guys. "Well hello, who are you three?" There's mock happiness in his face and I'm sure it's because he's being protective of me, but hell never say anything about me hanging out with guys.

"That's Will, Zach, and that's AssWhole." I say pointing at them all and grinning when I get to Blake.

"My name's Blake." He grunts out not too happy at being called Asswhole.

My dad makes no comment about me swearing, "Nice to meet you then." My dad replies before turning us back on them to face me and Ace. "We have family pictures tomorrow ." He informs me and I roll my eyes, "Tamara wants to take you two shopping to get clothes for it."

Tamara is my dad's wife and the mother of my two younger siblings, Aaron and Abbey; yes my father named all his children something that starts with an A. I think Aaron and Abbey are around thirteen and fourteen, I'm not sure considering the fact I've only seen and talked to them a handful of times.

"Where's Abbey and Aaron?" I ask my dad raising a brow.

"Yea," Ace says crossing his arms over his chest, "I haven't seen them since I've been here."

"They're away on a trip for their school but they'll be getting back at an hours top." He tells me, "You can go pick them up if you want, it'll be a good surprise for them since you haven't seen them in a while."

Of course they're away on a trip with their school. Abbey and Aaron attend one of those rich snobby private schools so I'm sure they probably visit places like the White House. I think the school starts accepting students in the fourth grade all the way through high school.

"Pick them up in what?" I ask my dad, "My cars back at home."

My dad rubs his chin in thought, "You can borrow the Audi if you want." He tells me.

Oh, my dad knows nice cars are my weakness.

"Okay," I say before realizing that means some people have to stay at home.

"Your friends can stay here and get use to the house while your away since they haven't been here before; with the exception of David and Jasmine." My father says as if reading my mind.

"Okay." I finally conclude, "Ace can drive since he knows his way around town better than I do." I say with a shrug even though I really want to drive the Audi.

"There's a GPS installed in it." My father tells me.

A grin makes its way onto my face "In that case where's the keys?"

"You've made it to your destination." The GPS says as I come to a stop at the school.

As I expected the school looks way nicer and at least ten times the size of my high school back at home. Dad gave us instructions to go into the main building and find the office there we can notify the office who we're here to pickup. Apparently all the students are waiting in the auditorium in the air for their rides to pick them up. Someone in the auditorium will notify them that their ride's here.

Ace and I make our way to the office as I wonder why he's living with dad again. He was staying with our grandma and grandpa and as far as I know they didn't pass away, so I'm quite curious.

Ace opens the door for me reminding me that he's quite the gentleman. I walk up to the front desk where a woman is typing away at her computer. She looks up at me with a forced smile.

"I'm picking up Aaron and Abbey Darling." I tell her.

"Okay, what relation to them do you have and please let me see your ID." Geez, I didn't realize we're playing detective.

I roll my eyes and pull out my ID, "I'm their sister." I tell her and she looks up at me in shock.

"The Darling kids have a sister?" She asks furrowing a brow as she goes to pull out a file.

"Uh yea," I tell her wondering why she's being so weird.

She opens the file and looks through it, "Hmm, they have a brother too." I hear her mutter.

"Yea, he's right here." I say pointing at Ace and she glances at him before putting away the files.

So they keep a file of their students whole family?

"Okay, I'll call Abbey out of the auditorium, Aaron is currently In the principal's office, he should be out in about five minutes, but I'll notify the principle that you're here."

She makes a couple of calls and Ace and I sit down on one of the benches that's located in the office. A couple of more parents come in to collect their kids and finally Abbey comes into the room. I know it's her because dad has some strong genes giving all his children the same Black hair and Blue eyes as him. Abbey looks how I looked when I was her age except she's taller than I was. The only differences that I can really tell between us is that her cheekbones are higher than mine and her eyebrows are thinner. She also wears more makeup than me.

She looks around the room before she sees us and a smile spreads across her face.

She runs up to us giving me a hug and then Ace, "Oh my gosh, I haven't seen you two in forever." She says In a happy mood.

"I know," Ace says with a smile, "I actually moved back in with dad, and Allison's here for the weekend."

The door beside our benches open and out walks and older lady with brown hair. Behind her is my delinquent brother and some girl who looks embarrassed.

She glances around and looks at Abbey and a smile comes onto her face, "Where's the people picking you two up?" She asks obviously not seeing Ae and I or not thinking we're here for these two.

"Right here." She says pointing at use and Aaron finally notices us, he lets out a breath of relief for some reason and gives us a nervous smile.

"Nice to meet you," The lady says and I'm guessing she's the principal, "What relationship do you have to the students?"

"We're their siblings." I tell her and she looks taken back.

Damn, why is everyone shocked to find we're related to them.

"Where do you go to school?" She asks.

"I go to school at RoseMary High, I just transferred so I start their next week." Ace says.

"And I go to school back home in Utah." I tell her.

"Are you twins?" She asks looking closely at us.

"No." We both say at the same time and she mutters something.

"Well your brother here is suspended from school for two days, and no longer has the privilege to go on school field trips out of state." She informs us pointing at Aaron.

"What did he do?" I ask trying my best not to smirk. Aaron has always been a trouble maker and Abbey's always been the sweet one.

"Why don't you tell them." The principal says looking at Aaron who gives us a half smile.

"I got caught with my phone."he says.

That's not even bad.

"Tell them the rest." The principal demands.

Aaron runs a hand through his hair, "And sexting." He admits and Ace looks at him in shock.

"You're not going to tell dad right?" Aaron asks from the backseat of the car.

"Of course not." I tell him.

"You know you're suspended, what are you going to say when you have to stay at home?" Ace asks disapprovingly.

"Tell dad your sick." I suggest to him knowing I've use that lie before.

"Good idea." Aaron says and Ace shoots me a glare.

"What, all he did was sext, people do it all the time, only he got caught." I defend him.

"Yea, and I wasn't the one sending the pictures, just receiving them." Aaron says in agreement.

"That's smart of you." I tell him, "You know people make those exposing pages now a days.." I cut my sentence off as Ace continues to glare at me.

Geez, I'm just giving my little brother advice.

"How was the trip?" My dad asks when we enter the house.

"Good." Aaron says before quickly going to his room.

"Hey dad, why are the lights in the guest house on?" Abbey asks Gavin dad a hug.

"Oh, Allison has some friends staying out there." He answers her.

Of course he stuck the guys in the guest house. It's his way of making sure I don't do anything with one if them, without just coming out and telling me not to.

"Your room is the way you left it last time, and Jasmine's in the guest room next to it that she usually stays in." My father tells me and I head upstairs while he talks to Ace.

Jasmine's in her guest room sitting on the bed watching TV. I can tell something's wrong with her and I'm pretty sure I know what it is.

"Seeing him brings back memories doesn't it?" I ask her closing the door to the room.

She looks at me and legs out a sigh, "Am I whore Allison?" She asks looking at me as I sit down on the bed.

I'm not sure if she's trying to avoid my question or what.

I smirk at her, "Yes."

She glares at me, "Yo were suppose to say no."

"I thought you wanted the truth." I tell her.

She rolls her eyes at me before her face softens, "Yes." She says not looking me in the eyes.

"Huh?"

"It brings back the memories when I see him and they hit me strong." She tells me, "When we first got here I was okay but I think it was because I was in shock of seeing him." She explains.

Ace grew up with us until dad moved to Malibu, Ace then went to live with him since his biological mother is dead. When we were about 13 dad agreed to let Ace move in with me and my mother since she's the closest thing to a mom that he has. Instead of going to school with us though Ace went to a different that wanted him to play sports for them. When Jasmine use to stay at our house they use to always good around and I thought it was because they never got to see each other until them. Well friendship soon turned into a friendship with benefits relationship. Jasmine lost her virginity to them and soon they were in love even though they were young and they started dating. About a year ago Ace had to leave to stay with our grandparents because dad wanted him closer to him. Obviously the two had to break up and when I say Jasmine went through hell I mean it. That's when she started hooking up and sleeping around a lot.

"That's not the only thing bugging you is it?" I ask looking her over.

She shakes her head, "It's Will too." She mutters and I hold back a smile.

"So are you finally going to tell me what's going on between you two?" I ask her.

"I should've known better from Ace." She says running a hand through her hair.

"You're doing the whole benefits thing again?" I ask her and she gives me a guilty look.

"Jasmine," I say letting out a groan.

"I know, I know, it wasn't even suppose to happen." She says.

"Explain." I say giving her a stern look.

"Well we hooked up the day that we were assigned that assignment." She says and my mouth drops open. The same day that the lemonade thing happened with Blake.

"So you guys arguing that day was just sexual tension."

She rolls her eyes, "You've got to listen. You know I have a rep about hooking up and so does he so I was quite curious about him." She says, "So stuff happened and soon I didn't want our hooking up to be a one time thing, we ended up sleeping together, and the sex was amazing."

"Get to the point." I tell her before she goes into more details.

She smirks at me, "So the night of our soccer game when he got jealous of that, guy he told me he thinks we should give us a try without just the sex and joking up." She tells me, "But I couldn't so I told him no." She says and now I know what's going on due to the years of knowing her so long.

"And now, you regret it don't you?" I ask her.

"Yes, you should him with girls at school flirting his ass off, I think he does it just to annoy me."

"Like how you hooked up with Zach just to annoy him?" I ask tilting my head.

"I was drunk," she says before something flashes in her eyes, "Speaking of that night and being drunk I know you've got some of your memories front that night back."

I know she's trying to get off the subject of herself and my face becoming red makes her continue.

"You do, don't you." She says smiling and I let out a nod.

Like usual when I get drunk and lose my memories they started to comeback to me over the week and I remember everything vividly.

"So how was it, is Blake as good as he's rumored to be?" She asks.

"Jasmine." I say running a hand through my hair, "I don't want to talk about it." I tell her.

"But it doesn't matter because we're going to." She tells me.

Just as I give in there's a knock at the door. I'm relieved while Jasmine looks pissed, "Come in?" She calls out to the person and the door opens.

When I see the person the relief floods from my face, "Can we talk?" Blake asks looking directly at me.

Chapter 23

I nervously walk into my room with Blake behind me soundlessly.

What does he want?

Blake closes the door behind him and I take a seat on my bed. For a while there's nothing but silence as we stare at each other. He looks calm but I can tell there's something bugging him.

Finally he lets out a deep breath interrupting our staring contest, "I'm Sorry." He mutters and my jaw drops open.

Blake's apologizing to me. Hell, I don't even know why he's doing it but its a shocker.

I gain control of my shock before speaking in a calm manner, "What for?" I ask curiously making eye contact once again.

He runs a hand through his hair nervously before glancing at the ground and finally making eye contact with me, "For you know.. Uh, deflowering you." He finally spits out.

So, that's what this is about?

"Deflowering me?" I raise a brow at him trying to hide the blush that's trying to form on my cheeks.

He nods his head, "Yea," he wipes his hands on his jeans and I know he's nervous, "For taking your virginity." He says.

I let out a sigh, "We were both wasted." I tell him looking at the ground.

"Well, I know girls usually want their first time to be special; and sleeping with a person you hate while at a party high, drugged, and drunk isn't the ideal special night." He says and I can't help but smile when I look up at him realizing he's closer than he was earlier. Now instead of standing by the door he's only a couple of feet away from me.

"I suppose that isn't the ideal night." I tell him running a hand through my hair.

He looks around the room before taking a deep breath and looking at me again. His clover eyes hold curiosity and something else that I can't quite define, "Do you, uh, remember anything now?" He finally asks as his eyes search my face.

I frown as I think about the memories that decided to make an appearance earlier this week. "Yea, I remember some parts" I tell him, "It was quite painful." I inform him.

He flinches a little bit at the last word but keeps a blank face, "I'm sorry, I thought since you were under the influence it wouldn't have really hurt, but I guess not."

I can't help but smile, "You know, you've apologized to me twice in the last fifteen minutes." I tell him and he frowns.

"Don't push your luck." He warns me and my smile brightens even more.

There's silence for a while as we just look at each other before Blake rubs his chin and tilts his head in thought. A smile makes it way onto his face, and I'm not talking about his usual smirk, no I mean a genuine smile and my heart starts to beat quicker.

Why the hell is his smile affecting me?

He moves a little closer to me, "I'm going to make it up to you." He finally says.

"Huh, how?" I ask looking up at him with a puzzled look on my face.

It's a shock that he wants to make it up to me for one, but how?

"I'm going to give you a redo of your first time." He says and my mouth drops open.

"What!" My eyes widen in shock, "And how in the hell are you going to do that?"

The smile on his face turns into a smirk, "Allison, I think we both know how sex works." Him saying my real name causes tingles through my body but I ignore it.

"And what makes you think I'm going to have sex with you?" I ask him crossing my arms over my chest.

"You did the last time." He says.

I just stare at him.

The smile returns to his face as he turns on his heel and makes his way to my door but before he leaves he turns around to look at me, "Don't worry I'll make sure you remember every single detail." He says and with that he leaves the room leaving me on my bed in shock.

Chapter 24

"Honey stop shaking your leg, your shaking the table." My father tells me taking a sip of his wine.

Right now my father, me, Ace, Abbey, Aaron, and Tamara are at dinner. We just got done shopping for our clothes for the photo shoot tomorrow. What Blake said has been running through my head all afternoon so I'm kind of nervous which is why my leg is shaking.

I frown before bringing my leg to a still and digging into my pasta. My dad frowns at me and I roll my eyes. Earlier he'd said that I don't act ladylike and I know me shoving my food into my mouth is exactly what he's talking about. This is why I live with my mom, my father and I can't agree on much.

"So," Tamara says plastering a smile onto her face, "How was the trip here Allison?" She asks wiping her hands on a paper towel.

"Horrible." I tell her.

"Were you not in first class?" She asks with a frown on her face.

"No." I tell her even though that isn't what made the trip horrible. It was an annoying pest named Blake.

"Oh, I thought that we'd gotten you first class tickets, my mistake." My father says with a frown on his face, "I'll make sure to get that fixed when you go back." He says.

A couple of girls who look around 14 walk by our table and Aaron gives them a wink causing them to giggle. I simply roll my eyes and Ace shakes his head.

Our dinner continues with awkward and forced conversations and soon we're on our way home. My friends had stayed at home since this was a "family" dinner. The limo -yes, limo- pulls up to the house letting us out at the front door. The Chauffeur opens our door and I'm the first to get out.

I make my way to the front door and pull it open heading straight to Jasmine's room. I'd told her earlier about Blake's redo but we couldn't continue to discuss it because of the "family" dinner. I pull her door open without knocking and find her watching TV.

"What now?" She practically yells but when she sees me her eyes light up, "Oh hey Allison?" She says as I raise a curious brow at her.

"What was with the freak out?" I ask.

"Oh nothing." She says just as someone walks in the room behind me.

I turn to see Will standing there. He looks between us awkwardly while Jasmine glares at him.

I guess that's who she thought I was...

"Uh.." I say awkwardly and Jasmine turns her attention to me.

"We'll talk later Alli." She says and I don't bother asking why knowing her and Will are probably going through their drama again.

I walk back into my room and with a sigh grab some night clothes. I may as well just go to sleep since there's nothing else to do in this house.

I'll think about Blake tomorrow.

I walk into my bathroom closing the door and placing my clothes on the counter. I strip out of all my clothes before stepping into the shower. Just as I'm washing my hair I hear the door open.

"Hey who's in here?" I call out but there's no reply.

Shit, I'm going to be killed in the shower of my day's million dollar mansion. At least I won't die as a virgin...

Just as I'm about to stick my head out of the shower I hear the door close. I let out a sigh.

Maybe it was just Jasmine coming in to borrow something.

I finish washing my hair before turning off the shower and stepping out. I grab two towels out of the cabinet, one for my hair, and one for my body. I wrap my hair off before wrapping one around my body. I open one of the drawers and find a blow dryer.

With a sigh I plug in the blow dryer before drying my hair. It comes out straighter than it would've if I just would've air or towel dryer it but its still a bit frizzy.

I go to the counter to pick up my clothes and frown when they're not there. No what's in the place of my nightclothes is lingerie. There's a black nightgown made of lace and has holes, which will leave not a lot to the imagination. There's also Lacey panties. My heart starts to beat quicker. Knowing I really have no other option I throw the lingerie on.

Once it's on I walk over to my mirror to examine myself. It looks like everything is only display even though I've clothes on. My skin sticks out through all of the holes and I frown. A scent starts to make its way into the bathroom and I can hear the introduction of a song. I debate wether to go check it out or not since I'm barely dressed. Deciding that I'm okay since no one is in my room I step out of the bathroom and my mouth drops open.

The lights in the room are off but there's lit blue candles all over the room. There's also blue flower petals on the bed. The words of the song start to play and I recognize the voice as Robin Thicke.

'Stressed out uptight, over worked wound up

Unleash what you got let's explore your naughty side'

"What do you think?" I gasp when I see Blake come into my line of view since bed been standing in an unlit part of the room, and I forget all about the song. He has on a pair of jeans but he has no shirt on so his abs are on full view and I just want to run my tongue over them.

I snap out of my dirty thoughts before looking at him in shock, "You did all this?" I ask him gesturing to the room.

He nods his head with a smirk on his face, "Jasmine helped a little." He says as he scans my body with his eyes.

I try to cover myself with my hands as I remember what I have on.

Blake shakes his head at me as he walks over to me. He pulls my hands away from my body and places them beside me, "Oh no, none of that tonight Allison." He says and my name rolls on his tongue in a husky seductive way.

The lyrics to the song start to seep into my head once again:

'It's your body you can yell if you want to

Loud if you want to, scream if you want to

Just let me love you lay right here girl don't be scared of me

Give you sex therapy, give you sex therapy

It's your body we'll go hard if you want to

As hard as you want to, soft as you want to

Just let me love you lay right here I'll be your fantasy

Give you sex therapy, give you sex therapy'

My face starts to redden a little and his smirk returns to his face as he runs his finger down my arm. He leans into me, "Tonight you're all mine SweetCheeks, and I'll have you begging me to take you higher than the Empire State Building." He says before leaning back and smashing his lips to mine.

For a second I don't respond because I'm In shock but it doesn't last long. I wrap my arms around his neck before deepening the kiss. Blake moves us and soon I'm on the bed on my back while he's on top of me. He pulls away from my mouth and moves onto my neck. Shivers run up and down my spine as his lips and tongue work miracles on my skin.

I run my hands over his muscled back and I almost panic when he starts to move down towards my breast that are out because of the lingerie. He looks up at me for a second before his tongue flicks out over one of them and my body starts to heat up.

I'm pretty sure he did this the first time but not all parts of that night are quite re memorable. I let out an involuntary moan when Blake starts to kiss me again. He slips his tongue into my mouth as his hands travel my body. He breaks the kiss again and I look up at him out of breath.

"You know I never agreed to this redo thing." I tell him.

He frowns moving his hands to the top of the nightgown, "Really?" He tilts his head to the side in thought, "Do you want me to stop then?" He asks.

"No." I tell him and the words barely out of my mouth before he rips the nightgown off of me. Once it's ripped all the way down the middle he throws it on the ground.

Now I'm laying down in nothing but my underwear that's not covering much and Blake still has on his jeans. He glances down at my body in awe -as if its the first time- and I blush even more. Trying to take the attention off of me I reach for his pants' button.

Blake catches my hands and shakes his head. "No, we're going to take this nice and slow Allison."

Chapter 25

I wake up to an arm draped over my torso and a leg thrown over mines. My whole body feels warm from both of our body heat. We're both naked but I don't feel awkward like I always thought I would the morning after sex.

I turn my head revealing a peacefully sleeping Blake. Thoughts start to run through my head:

Why did I let him sleep with me, again?

Why don't I feel any dislike towards him anymore?

Why did he offer to give me a redo?

I sigh forgetting all about my thoughts not wanting to ruin my day since I actually feel happy, oddly enough. I try to remove one of Blake's leg but he starts to stir when I do.

Deciding to go back to sleep since I feel a bit tired I doze back off.

Something light trails across my face and my eyes flutter open. The first thing I see is Blake's green eyes. His hand is on my cheek but he instantly removes it.

"Morning," he says to me with a smile on his face.

I smile back at him, "GoodMorning." I sit up on the bed bringing the sheets with me to keep my body covered. Blake sits up not bothering to cover his chest.

There's a comfortable silence for a while until I break it, "So you have a thing for Robin Thicke, huh?" I ask recalling the day he was singing blurred lines in the car, and last night.

His smile widens as he trails a finger along my arm causing me to shiver. "You've got to admit, it kind of set the mood." He says.

I roll my eyes at him, before slowly getting out of the bed. I feel a pain between my legs and wince as I slip on underwear.

"Are you okay?" Blake asks coming around the bed to stand in front of me.

"Yea, I'm fine just a little sore..." My sentence trails off as I ran my eyes up and down his still naked body.

Blake smirks when he sees my eyes wondering, "Stop looking at me like that," he says raising my chin so I'm looking at his face, "because as much as I want to sleep with you again you're sore and I don't want for you to be hurt even more."

I blush a bit before his words really sink in.

He doesn't want to hurt me?

What has happened to the Blake I've come to dislike?

There's a knock on the door breaking us out of our silence. I turn my head, "Who is it?" I call out grabbing my robe.

"Ace!" The person calls out and I almost have a heart attack.

My eyes widen when I glance at Blake. I push him into the bathroom before slipping my robe on and opening my door a bit flushed.

"Yes?" I ask opening the door wide enough so that I can only stick my head out.

Ace raises a brow at me, "Breakfast is almost ready." He says skeptically frowning at me.

"Okay," I tell him before quickly closing the door in his face.

I let out a sigh of relief just as Blake comes out of the bathroom. "Did you really have to shove me?" He asks picking up his boxers off the floor and slipping them on.

"Yea, I didn't want my brother to see you." I tell him.

"I get that a lot," he says indicating how many people he's slept with and had to hide from their family.

I glare at him and he smirks going back to his usual arrogant self. He slips on his jeans buttoning them up.

"Well I'll see you at breakfast." He says before grabbing me by my waist and pulling me into him giving me a long kiss that I can't help but respond to. "Bye Allison." He whispers in my ear sending shivers through me before leaving the room.

I let out a grunt after he leaves running a hand through my hair.

What in the hell have I gotten myself into?

I trudge down the stairs after having a shower and slipping on some clothes. I feel happier than I did earlier after Blake left my room which I suppose is good.

Everyone's sitting at the table in the dinning room with plates in front of them. I take the empty seat between Jasmine and Ace, where a plate of eggs, bacon, and pancakes are.

"So how was your night?" Jasmine asks me with a mischievous smile on her face and everyone turn their attention to us. I lift my eyes up to see Blake smirking at me.

I bet I can fix his ego.

"It was okay," I say nonchalantly sprinkling salt on my eggs, "It could've been better."

I look at Blake who's glaring at me and a smile makes its way onto my face.

Ha I bet he doesn't feel so confident anymore.

"So how was it actually?" Jasmine asks me as we're at the photo shoot waiting for our "family" pictures to be done. Right now Tamara and Dad are taking pictures together.

I look at Jasmine knowing exactly what she's talking about but I avoid the question, "You know, you could've gave me a heads up." I tell her frowning.

"Yea, yea, but then it wouldn't have been a surprise and everything would've been ruined." She tells me. "So answer my question how was it?" She asks.

"Okay," I say casually trying to downplay every thing.

She raises a brow at me, "On a scale from one to ten?" She asks.

I sigh knowing I can't really lie to hear, "A 100," I answer and she lets out a girly squeal causing me to roll my eyes.

"So was it slow, or did you just fuck hard?" She asks causing a blush on my face.

"Which time?" I ask smirking at her.

"Time?" She questions as a smile appears on her face, "How many times did you guys do it?" She asks.

I try to remember but I really can't.

"Five." Blake says appearing behind us scaring us both. "I think, it may have been more than that." He says with a satisfied smile and I hope he didn't hear the part about the sex being a 100, "I think we stopped after Allison couldn't take anymore."

Jasmine claps her hands together happily, "So are you two," she points at us, "you know.. Together now?" She asks.

"No," I tell her with a glare.

Blake smiles, amusement twinkling in his eyes, "Really, I thought we had something Sweet Cheeks."

Jasmine gets up and leaves us alone on purpose.

"No we've nothing Blake." I tell him as he sits next to me.

"Really, because I'm pretty sure rating our sex a 100 means something," he says smirking, "I'm also pretty sure it means you want to do it again." He says.

"No, it's not going to happen again." I tell him.

"We'll see."

I roll my eyes at him just as my dad informs us that it's time fore the children to join the picture. I sigh as I slide in between Aaron and Abbey for the picture. We take a lot of pictures from different angles before dad announces he has business to tend to and him and Tamara leaves. Abbey, Ace, Aaron, and I pose for a couple of more pictures, before Jasmine suggests we all get some together, it'll all be charged to my day's card anyway and I'm sure he won't say anything.

Jasmine and I pose for a couple of pictures together with David before we take different ones. Everyone watches though as Jasmine pushes both Blake and I in front of the camera.

It's like they all know we slept together.

I've no doubt that Will knows but I'm not sure about everyone else.

"Smile big SweetCheeks." Blake says throwing his arm over my shoulder and I can't help but smile just as the camera flashes.

We return home and I'm sad to leave Ace but he promised to come visit. As promised mom got my car fixed so Blake and I don't have to ride together anymore which is good. Weeks pass by as some things return to normal while others don't. Mom and Blake's mom continue to go out but their gambling habits have become critical and they tend to lose lots of money. Blake goes back to being a man whore and leaving me alone besides the occasional flirting while in class. Jasmine and Will are still arguing. We've been winning all of our soccer games. I haven't heard from Zach since we went out of town.

I myself have been feeling different. Well it's more like someone making me feel different. That someone being a player named Blake. Lately, I can't help but start to blush, and feel butterflies in my stomach when he's around. I haven't hooked up a lot lately either since it just doesn't feel right. I can't help but feel a twinge if jealousy when I see Blake with other girls. I also can't help watching him sometimes but sometimes I find he's doing the same thing to me.

Needless to say everything's been complicated.

And to add to that homecoming is coming up.

"Uh, I'll think about it." I tell yet another guy who's asked me out to home coming.

"Okay," he says with a grin before walking away.

Jasmine shakes her head at me, "What's that, the fifth one today?" She asks leaning against her locker.

"Fifth what?" David asks appearing in front of us.

"Person, who's asked me out." I tell him with a groan slamming my locker door closed.

"Poor you," he says smirking, "I've already got a date." He tells me.

"Who?" I ask raising a brow at him, "Wilma Banks." He says with a satisfied smile.

I roll my eyes since everyone knows Wilma is a whore.

"Yay you," I say resting my head against my locker, "I just don't find any of the guys around here appealing enough to go with." I say.

"Well considering you and Jasmine have hooked up with half of the school you would think you would've found someone." He says earning a punch from Jasmine.

"Well at least I haven't slept with all of them like Wilma." I say.

"Yea," Jasmine says, "Do you know how many diseases your going to get from her."

"I use protection so it doesn't matter." He says, "So of you guys would excuse me," he says looking at his watch, "I have a quickie set up for nine in the boy's. bathroom and it is now 8:15." With that he walks away leaving us.

I close my eyes as my stomach begins to hurt like it has for a while now, "Are you okay?" Jasmine asks.

"Yea, my stomach just hu-" I can't even get the rest of my sentence out before I'm running to the bathroom to vomit.

Jasmine holds my hair as I spill my guts out. I'm finally able to stop so sit on the bathroom floor with my head in my hands.

"Alli Babe," Jasmine says with a frown in her face, "You've been throwing up a lot lately." She says, "And I've noticed you've been burning energy faster than usual." She says.

"Yea, I'll be fine." I tell her with a wave if my hand.

She pulls a bottle of water out of her purse and passes it to me.

"No, there's something wrong honey." She says standing up making sure no one's in the bathroom with us before locking the door.

She squats down in front of me again, "When was your last period honey?" She asks concerned etched on her face.

I frown as I try to remember my last period, "I don't know." I admit.

"So you're late?" She asks.

"Yea," I say running a hand through my hair.

She sighs, "Think real hard, when you and Blake had sex did you use protection?" She asks.

"Uh, which time?" I ask her.

"Allison, every time." She says.

"Uh, I'm not sure." I tell her and she runs her hands through her hair in frustration muttering curse words under her breath.

"Allison, honey, I think you're pregnant."

Chapter 26

No, there's no way I'm pregnant. I can't be.

I look up at Jasmine who has an apologetic look on her face, "I'm sorry babe," she says grabbing my hands to pull me up from the floor, "you have to tell Blake." She says.

I shake my head at her, "I don't because we're not sure if I am." I tell her.

"But there's a possibility so you need to be honest with him." She tells me running a hand through her hair.

I turn to the sink to wash my hands but I feel like breaking down. Being pregnant will ruin my whole life.

"Can't we just go buy a test?" I ask her.

"I think you should go to a clinic to see."she suggest.

"Okay, we can go later." I tell her, "But right now I need to get to class," I tell her.

"Allison, I'm serious." She says and I dismiss her with a wave of my hand.

"So am I," I tell her as we leave the restroom,"Lets just drop it for now, I don't need anymore stress." I say with a sigh.

"Okay," she says finally letting it drop.

"To the goal Allison!" Coach yells at me banging on his clip board.

Adrenaline runs through my body as I shove through the defense to get to the goal. I rear my leg back before sending the ball right at the goal. Unfortunately the goalie catches the ball making me swear.

"Allison!" Coach yells but I ignore him as I try to get the ball back from the opposing team.

I finally get it back but instead of taking the shot again I pass the ball to one of my team members. I'm so tired that I can't even make it back to the goal. I bend over with my hands on my knees trying to catch my breath.

"Allison, what do you think you're doing?" Coach yells running up the sidelines until he's standing on the edge by where I am. "Get your ass back into the game now!" He yells at me.

"O-okay," I say standing up straight taking a deep breath before forcing my self to run to the goal.

"Are you okay?" Jasmine asks jogging over to me when we're lining back up since the other team scored.

"N-no," I tell her as my eyes start to water.

My stomach hurts and my chest feels like its about to just shatter inside of me.

"Coach sub!" Jasmine yells as she places her arm over my shoulder to support me since if I try to stand on my own I'll probably fall out.

"What do you mean, sub?" He yells with fire in his eyes, "Darling's fine, get back in the game!" He looks like he's ready to rip me a new one.

"Take a knee," Jasmine says to me through clenched teeth and she looks like she's ready to just punch Coach in the face.

I know she wants me to take a knee because the refs will have to stop the game, and they'll take me out.

I slowly get down on one knee and eventually I hear the whistle blow. The rest of the players on the field take a knee and coaches come rushing into the field except Coach Lee: he simply standing on the sidelines with his arms crossed over his chest and a glare on his face.

"What's Wrong?" Coach Miles asks with a worried look on his face.

"Stomach." I say managing to get the one word out before I lay down on the ground. It's even taking too much energy to sit up right now.

"What else?" I hear coach asks and I bring a hand to my throat, "You can't breath?" He asks and I nod my head.

"She has to come out." I hear one of the refs say, "it's part of the sports administration policy."

"Okay," Coach Miles says putting a hand under my back to lift me up,"get up really slowly." He says and I do as he says.

The coaches escort me off the field to the sidelines and I sit on the bench as a freshman goes to buy me a Gatorade. Coach Lee simply glares at me.

"So, we lost today." Coach Lee says with disgust after the game.

That's right, we've lost our first game for this season.

He glares at the whole team and shakes his head, "I've nothing to say to you all, just get out of my presence." He says acting like a drama queen.

I roll my eyes as he dismisses everyone grabbing his things and leaving without another word.

Jasmine walks over to me with sweat dripping down her forehead, "Are you okay?" She asks and I nod.

"Here Freshy," she says tossing my bag at one of the freshman, "Help is out to her car." The freshman nods her head and Jasmine wraps her arm around me to help me stand up.

She leans into me as we're walking to the car, "You really need to get to a doctor." She whispers harshly.

"Agreed." A husky familiar voice says from behind us and my face heats up. We turn around to see Blake and Will. Will looks like he's high while Blake looks upset.

He doesn't know, does he?

Jasmine glances at me and there's panic on his face.

My eyes widen for a second at the thought of Blake knowing I could be pregnant.

"You may have some kind if virus or something and I don't want to get it." He says wrinkling his nose up and I take a deep bath.

"We wouldn't want that happening now would we?" I ask sarcastically and he smirks.

"I'll drive you home," he says taking a step closer to me causing my body to heat up. He glances at Jasmine, "I've got her." He says wrapping an arm around my waist to support me.

"Okay." Jasmine says drawing out the word.

"Well I'll take your car then since your my ride." She says getting my bag from the freshman to get my car keys out.

"In that case you can take me home." Will says with a goofy grin on his face.

Jasmine squints her eyes at him, "Are you high?" She asks.

"Only high on you babe," he says smiling wider and taking a step towards her.

"Maybe we should get out of here before start World War three." Blake says taking my bag from the freshman and leading me to his car.

I feel light headed from our closeness and there's butterflies in my stom-ach. He helps me into the car as if he's an actual gentleman, and throws my bag into the backseat.

After he's in the driver's seat he starts the car and turns on the radio. "So.." He says after there's a while of silence.

"So what?" I ask glancing at him and he glances at me.

He runs a hand through his hair, "Homecoming's next week, are you going?" H asks and my heartbeat speeds up.

"Uh yea," I say, "Are you going?"

"Yea," he answers glancing over at me before looking back at the road, "Who are you going with?"

Why does it matter to him?

"Why?" I ask watching him.

His hands clench on the wheel but he keeps his face blank, "Just wondering." He finally says and I know that's not the full truth.

I shrug my shoulders closing my eyes and leaning my head on the seat, "NoOne, yet." I answer as I relax against the seat.

"Really?" He sounds shocked, "Hasn't someone asked you?" He asks and I feel his gaze on me so I open my eyes to look at him.

"Eyes back on the road." I tell him and he obeys, before I go back to leaning against the seat and closing my eyes, "Of course I've had people ask me, there's been bunches." I admit.

"And you rejected them?" He asks and there's something in his tone. I can't unite place it but it sounds like relief.

That's weird.

"Not exactly." I tell him.

"What do you mean not exactly?" He asks and I feel his eyes on me again.

"I keep telling them I'll think about it or get back to them." I answer.

"You know, you're really leading them on." He says and it reminds me of the day we were at Jasmine's house and he said the same thing, when he had me a whore the night before.

Still feeling his eyes on me I open my own and realize we're at my house.

I hadn't even felt the car stop.

"I don't think of it as leading them on," I tell him, "More of sparing their feelings." He nods his head before walking around the car to help me out.

"I think I can stand on my own," I tell him since I feel a little better now.

"I think I'll still help you," he say grabbing my bad before wrapping his arm around my waist.

I simply roll my eyes at him knowing if I argue he'll just end up winning.

He doesn't let go of me until we get upstairs to my room and find a note on my bed:

Gone out of town of a week with Beatrice. We'll be back Friday.

Leaving the house to you and Blake.

No parties and stay safe.

-mom

You've got to be kidding me.

"Looks like I'm staying the night," Blake says smirking at me as he sits my things down on the floor by my bed.

"Uh no," I say crossing my arms over my chest.

"Why not?" He ask with smirk still remaining on his face, "Afraid you're gong to give into my good looks, and fu-"

"Shut up." I say as a blush comes onto my face.

"It's the truth isn't it?" He asks with a satisfied smile on his face.

"No," I say sitting down on my bed not looking at him as I turn the TV on.

"I'm going to run by my house and get some clothes," he says but I don't look at him still, "Maybe by then you won't still want to jump my bones."

Before I can reply to him he's out the door and I hear his laughter echoing through the halls.

While waiting for Blake to get back I go downstairs to fix me something to eat. I end up throwing some chicken strips in the oven. I eat three of them leaving the rest on the stove since I know Blake will come in complaining if I didn't fix him some.

As I'm making my way back to my room the urge to vomit overwhelms and I run to the bathroom. After I'm done I stay sitting by toilet since I don't have enough energy to stand up.

"SweetCheeks!" I hear Blake call out as he comes up the stairs but I'm too exhausted to answer him. He walks by the bathroom as he's on his way to my room but he stops when he sees me sitting in the bathroom. He frowns before dropping a bag he was carrying and rushing over to me, "Are you okay?" He asks.

I let out an unamused snort, "What does it look like to you?" I ask sarcastically.

"Always the smart ass," he mutters before sliding his arms underneath me and picking me up bridal style. If I wasn't so sick I'd probably be swooning over him right now.

He carries me all the way to my room placing me on my bed gently.

"I'll be back," he says before leaving the room and he re enters with a bottle of water. "Here," he passes it to me.

"Thanks," I say after taking a couple of sips.

"Do you think you're going to be okay for tonight?" He asks and I give him a weak shrug.

He looks at me for a second as conflict passes through his face. He looks at the door before letting out a sigh and closing it.

"What are you doing?" I ask as he kicks his shoes off and strips down to nothing but his boxers. He turns out the light leaving the TV as the only source of light in the room.

He slides into bed next to me, "I'm staying with you," he says wrapping an arm around me and letting me snuggle into his chest.

"Why?" I ask looking up into his eyes.

He looks back at me and I can't describe what his facial expression is giving away but it's definately soft.

"I don't know," he answers before I doze off to sleep.

For a week now I've been feeling and looking like a zombie. I keep vomiting a lot and my energy is down. Coach has been blaming me for our first lost and I'm really starting to feel like I let the team down. Blake's been around more often lately. My mom and Beatrice still aren't back, they called the other day saying they blew all of their money for a ride back home. On top of that mom got fired for never coming into work. All in all I'm becoming even more stressed.

Today's homecoming and I finally said yes to some guy named Eric. I really don't know him to well, but he's cute enough so oh well.

"You look pretty," Jasmine says glancing at me when I get to homecoming, "Well compared to how you've been looking all week, you look pretty." She says.

"Well thanks," I say sarcastically, "you just make a girl feel really special."

"I know," she says, "I'm going to go dance now, so see you later." She tells me as she drags her date to the dancefloor.

The gymnasium is decorated in purple and green, it looks really horrible. I've no idea who was over the decorations but they seriously need their ass kicked for this tacky scenery.

"Do you want to dance?" Eric asks running a hand through his blond hair.

"I'd rather not," I tell him walking away to grab a drink and sit down.

As I'm sitting down Eric goes to talk to one of his friends and I debate leaving. I really don't want to be here, it's boring and I don't feel good. On top of that Blake's here with som girl and I feel jealous.

"Who's that guy that Jasmine's with?" Will asks as he slips into one of the seats at my table nodding in the direction of Jasmine and her date.

I try to rack my brain for the guy's name but I can't really remember, "I don't know, some college guy, that goes to school with her cousin." I tell him and he looks like he's about to have a heart attack.

"Cheater," I hear him mutter under his breath before his date comes ver to the table frowning at him, "What?" He asks her in a bitter tone.

Well someone's pissed

"I want to dance," she says.

"Then go dance," he says with a wave of his hand as he sits back in his chair with his arms folded over his chest.

The girls stomps aways pouting and Will remains in his sea glaring at Jasmine. About 15 minutes later Blake, his date, Jasmine, her date, and Eric have made their way to our table. I think there's a couple of more people but I don't know or care since my head's down on the table.

"I'm going to the bathroom," I finally mutter and Eric offers to walk me there. As we're leaving I see Blake send a glare our way.

Ugh, what's his problem now?

We're barely by the bathroom before Eric spins me around and pushes me into a janitor's closet, hard. He forces his lips on mine and I try to fight him off. He pulls away and his alcohol breath hits me hard.

"Stop!" I yell at him as he tries to pull my dress off.

If this were any other day and I wasn't feeling so bad I'd probably be all to fight him off but today I don't have a chance.

"Shut up!" He hisses as he slaps me and I cry out.

I hear footsteps in the hallway and I start yelling loudly before he clamps a hand over my mouth.

"Oh my god," someone yells when they open the door. I can tell its a girl and the voice sounds slightly familiar.

When I look up I see that it's Megan, "Help!" She yells loudly as she tries to pull Eric off of me.

"Hey what's wrong?" I hear a male voice asks.

"Help!" Megan shouts at him as Eric tries to shut her up by shoving her down and trying to run.

I watch as he falls to the ground and the guy who must've asked what's wrong keeps him pinned there.

He looks at Megan telling her to go get a teacher. I just stay where I am as tears start to run down my face.

Soon there's a lot of students in the hallway along with chaperones and teachers.

Someone's wrapped a jacket around me and the counselor's holding me in a firm grip as I cry.

A hand touches my back and I flinch. "Shit." I hear them swear and I know it's Blake. I turn around and burry myself into him he wraps his arms around me as David, Will, and Jasmine comes over to us.

"He didn't, did he?" Jasmine asks and I know what she's implying.

"He tried," I manage to get out as more tears run down my face.

The teachers are holding the guy down and I feel Blake pull away from me a little. He gently pulls me away from him and shoves me into Will's arms who wraps his arms around me. "Blake, don't." He says sharply but it's too late Blake's already ripped Eric out of the teachers's hold.

He throws him onto the ground before repeatedly punching him in the face. It takes the football coach and two football players to pull Blake off of him and he still ends up kicking the guy until he's fully dragged away from him.

For some reason this makes me cry harder.

"It's okay," Will says running a hand through my hair in a comforting motion.

"Let go of me," Blake shouts breaking free of the people. Instead f going back to beating the shit out of Eric -who's really bloody- he comes over to me and grab me gently. "Come on," he whispers to me wrapping a protective arm over me and I follow him to his car. I've no idea what hale need I his date but it doesn't seem that he cares.

He helps me into the car with his teeth clenched, "I should've checked on you." He says as he presses down on the gas, and clutch the wheel harder,

"This is all my fault." He continues to ramble, "I knew there was something up with that guy."

"It wasn't your fault," I say softly wiping away some of my tears. I look over at him and think about what Jasmine said last week.

I really need to tell him.

"It is my faul-," he's cut short by my next words.

"I think I'm pregnant."

Chapter 27

"Is it mine?" Are the first words out of Blake's mouth and to say that pisses me off would be an understatement.

My eyes widen as I look at him, "Did you really just ask me that?" I say with a glare. I don't even wait for his answers as I fling the door open and get out of the car since we're already at my house.

How, dare he ask me if its his, who else does he think I had sex with.

Asswhole.

"Allison, you know I didn't mean it like that!" He calls out after me as he follows me into the house and I remember he's staying with me since our moms are still out of town.

I ignore him as I continue making my way to my room and slamming the door in anger.

That Jerk.

He knows damn well he's the only guy I've slept with. I mean, really who asks that. Is it his? Geez I could kill him.

I strip out of my dress and shiver when I remember what happened with Eric. I throw my heels off before walking over to my dresser to get out some shorts and a tank top.

My door slams open as I'm going through my dresser. I turn to see that Blake is staring at me, well my body.

"What?" I ask crossing my arms over my chest as I try to ignore the fact that I'm in only my panties and underwear while Blake looks at me.

Its not like he hasn't seen me in less.

"Allison," He says finally looking at my face, "You know I didn't mean it when I asked if it was mine," He tells me taking a couple of more steps into the room. "I was just in shock." He runs a hand through his hair in frustration.

"Did you use protection?" I ask him since Jasmine had brought it up.

He has a thoughtful look on his face before he frowns.

Oh hell.

"So why are you here today Mrs. Darling?" The doctor asks me as she glances at me and Blake.

"Well, I think I may be pregnant." I tell her and she nods her head.

"Okay," she says looking at the file again, "A couple of mandatory ques-tions." She says as she sits down in front of us on a stool.

"Alright," I tell her as I try to relax in my chair.

"Do you smoke?" She asks me.

"No."

"Do any drugs?"

"No."

"Drink?"

Dammit, I can't lie.

"Yes."

"Have you had sex before?"

Obviously, if I think I'm pregnant.

"Yes."

"How many partners?"

I take a glance at Blake before answering, "One."

She asks a couple of more questions before leaving the room to go get a bottle for me to pee in.

I glance at Blake who looks like he's about to pass out.

"You're not the one whose body has to go through all the changes." I tell him with a glare.

"Yea, but I'm too young to be a daddy." He says and I narrow my eyes at him. He holds his hands up in surrender, "Hey, don't get me wrong, if you are pregnant; I'll be there for you one hundred percent." He says and I let out a breath of relief.

Maybe it's bad but every since Jasmine brought up the possibility of me being pregnant, I've been thinking Blake will bail. It makes me feel better that he'll be here through everything.

Blake frowns as he watches my face, "Did you really think I would just bail on you Allison?"

Uh oh, he just said my real name meaning he's being serious.

I'm saved from having to answer him when the doctor comes back in with the little bottle for me to pee in. She doesn't even say anything before I've grabbed it and make my way straight to the bathroom.

"Okay, it shouldn't take any longer than five minutes." She tells me when I come back out of the bathroom and pass her the bottle.

"Great." I say and she leaves the room once again.

I take my seat next to Blake again and try to avoid eye contact.

"You didn't answer me." He says finally breaking the silence.

I let out a sigh knowing he's not going to let me avoid this question.

"Yes." I finally tell him.

"Really, Allison?" he asks and I nod.

"I would never, I may be an ass sometimes, but I wouldn't just leave you with a baby that I helped make." He says and I look at him to see that he's being sincere.

We sit in silence watching the clock as we wait for the doctor and she finally comes in. "Well we've got the results."

Chapter 28

"You're not pregnant," The doctor says as she sits down across from me and Blake once again, she gives me a light smile, "The test came back negative."

I let out a relieved sigh and Blake wraps his arm around my shoulder and I can't help but lean into him since its comforting.

"You told me you've been vomiting, losing energy, and missing your cycles." She says with a worried look on her face.

"Yes," I confirm.

"I really recommend you go see your regular doctor, but I must ask; have you been under a lot of stress lately?" She crosses her leg over the other as she looks at me.

I shrug my shoulders as I think about everything that's been happening, and I know I am under a lot of stress, "Yea." I tell her.

"Well, I'm going to say that's what your problem is," she says with a shake of her head, "but really go see your doctor, stress can take a real toll on you physically and mentally."

After leaving the clinic Blake and I go to get something to eat. The doctor wrote me a prescription for birth control so we've already dropped it off at the pharmacy.

"You know you would think that you would remember to use protection." I tell Blake as we're sitting down at McDonald's eating.

He glares at me before stealing one of my fries, "You should've reminded me." He shoots back at me.

I simply narrow my eyes at him.

Looks like we're back to arguing...

"You're the one who's suppose to take care of that," I argue stealing one of his fries to replace mines that he took, "Plus, I was intoxicated the first time and you surprised me the second time." I tell him.

"Well," he says with a smirk, "I was trying to make the second time special and I hate wearing condoms it takes away from the whole thing."

He did not just say that in a public place.

I look to my left to see that an elderly couple are frowning at us.

"Will you shush," I tell him with a shake of my head as I try to avoid the stares of people looking at us.

"Why?" He asks with a smirk leaning back in his seat with a playful gleam in his eyes, "Do you not like talking about my dick, I thought you're mouth was very fond of it."

My eyes widen at his words and the elderly couple begin to gather their things to leave.

"Blake!" I shriek kicking him under the table and he simply laughs. I lean across the table frowning at him, "I didn't even put my mouth on it." I mutter.

He shoots me a smile as he picks up my shake, "I know but the look on their face," he points at the elderly couple through the window who are hurrying to get into their old car, "was priceless."

I just shake my head at him and watch as he drinks my shake, "buy me another one," I tell him.

He frowns at me, "why?"

"Because you just drunk all of mine," I tell him and he grumbles something but goes to the register to order something as I clean up our table since he doesn't bother throwing away his trash.

Once I'm done clearing the table I walk to the register where the cashier is flirting with Blake who's leaning against the counter flirting right back. I feel a twinge of something in my stomach and I hate that I know it's nothing other than jealousy. I try to ignore and I'm happy when the shake finally comes out because now we can leave but my happiness drops when the cashier writes her number down on the customer receipt for Blake; he gives her a wink before we leave.

When Monday finally rolls around I get a lot of stares and I know it's because of homecoming night. At some point in the day I'm called to the counselor's office to make sure I'm "okay." I'm happy when it's finally gym time because its the last class of the day and I can actually have fun.

Unfortunately everything gun about PE disappears when I see Blake talking to Mercedes. To make matters worst Coach Miles is glaring at me from across the court.

"Hey just ignore everyone," Jasmine tells me nudging my shoulder as we walk to the bleachers.

"I have no idea what you're talking about, I'm fine." I grumble plopping down on the bleachers.

Jasmine sits next to me and her eyes wonder across to the gym where Blake is leaning against the bleachers and Mercedes is standing in front of him talking and touching his arms.

Bitch.

"You're jealous, it's fine," Jasmine says with amusement in her eyes, "Blake isn't into Mercedes anyways."

"I can't tell from the way he's smiling and laughing." I tell her.

She rolls her eyes, "Just a hint when a guy is with another girl but he's looking at you he's more than likely trying to make you jealous." She tells me.

What?

Blake isn't looking at me...

I lift my eyes to see that Blake is indeed actually looking at me. Well he keeps glancing this way. Our eyes meet and a smirk slowly makes its way onto his face.

Oh hell, I know that smirk.

He's up to something.

Blake looks down at Mercedes sending her a bright smile. Even from where I'm sitting I can hear Mercedes giggling as Blake says something to her. He runs a hand down her arm and I want to rip that arm off so much I start to grit my teeth.

"Hey Mercedes I think there's something red on the back of your pants!" Jasmine yells across the gym from beside me.

Mercedes turns around and sends a glare our ya as people start to laugh.

"Oh sorry, is it your time of the month?" Jasmine calls out in an innocent voice as if she didn't know what she was doing.

Mercedes flips Jasmine the middle finger before stomping off to the bathroom.

"Aren't I just the greatest best friend ever?" Jasmine says nudging me and I roll my eyes.

As I make my way to my car after PE Blake brushes by me but instead of just walking by he leans down to whisper in my ear, "You know if you don't want me hanging around other girls all you have to do is admit that you like me and I'll quit," he leans back and winks at me, "Jealousy is an ugly thing SweetCheeks." With those words he walks away to his car.

Chapter 29

B lake is an ass.

I rip apart a sheet of paper as I think about what he said after school. I mean really he's just a...

Ugh.

He's everything.

An ass.

A jerk.

A pain in my ass.

But yet he's proved that he actually has a sweet side to him. Only on rare occasions, but all the same he's sweet to me sometimes.

What puzzles me is his statement about knowing I like him:

'You know if you don't want me hanging around other girls all you have to do is admit that you like me and I'll quit.'

He said that and then he winked.

He's just a confusing, sometimes sweet Asswhole.

Yes, that's what he is.

The door to my room opens and I look up to see the devil himself smiling at me.

He looks at all the pieces op paper around my room that I've been ripping up every since I got home. Considering I got home at three and it's now six that's a lot of paper.

"Looks like you've had a lot on your mind." He says with a smirk and I know he's taunting me.

"What?" I ask crossing my arms over my chest.

"I'm going out, want to come?" He asks.

"Where to?"

He rolls his eyes at me as he leans against my door, "does it matter?"

"Yes," I tell him even though it obviously doesn't.

"Oh well because I'm not telling you, get dressed so we can go." He tells me before walking out of the door.

"I thought you were giving me an option!" I call out to him as I stand up to close my door so I can get dress.

"Well I chose for you!"

I roll my eyes slamming my door.

Our moms still aren't back which is why Blake is still at my house. I mean how could they have possibly gambled their money they were suppose to be using to get back home. I mean really if they can't even afford a way home how are they going to pay rent? Those two women seriously act like they're rebellious teenagers.

I let out a sigh as I realize I'll probably have to get my dad to wore me money so I can fly their asses back home.

Forgetting about my thoughts I start to rummage through my dressers for something to wear. Since I don't know where Blake's taking me I have no idea what to wear, but knowing him it's probably somewhere wild so I shouldn't dress to classy.

I end up picking out black jean shorts, and a blue tank top.

Hmmm, what shoes?

I end up putting on a pair of blue flip flops.

"Hurry up, I'm waiting in the car!" Blake calls out from downstairs and a second later I hear the front door slam.

I throw on just tiniest bit of makeup before letting my hair fall in waves around my shoulders. As I'm doing a once over I hear Blake blowing his car horn repeatedly.

Ass.

I roll my eyes before hurrying to the car. I get in and slam the car door but instead of fussing like he would usually do Blake looks at me. He takes me in from head to toe -at least the best way you can while in a car.-

We both speak at the same time.

"What?"

"Why are you wearing that?"

Obviously the last statement came from Blake.

I roll my eyes at him.

I can wear whatever I want to wear.

"Because we're going out." I say.

"Well aren't your shorts just a little too short?"

Is he serious?

"Uh no, why do you care anyway."

He doesn't answer me, he simply looks at me before pulling out of the driveway.

Loser.

We finally reach our destination and its a two story house with music blasting from it. We're on a whole different side of town though, this is where there's always shootings and killings on the news.

What in the hell is he thinking bringing me here.

"Blake -,"

He shakes his head cutting me off, "If I thought that you were in any type of danger I wouldn't bring you here." He says replying to my unspoken statement.

"Though I do recommend staying away from anything that isn't in a can unless you want to wake up in some random guys bed; I think you don't want to do that when you can come get in my bed any time." With those last words he gets out of the car and walks toward the house leaving me alone.

With a grunt I get out of the car slamming the door shut behind me. A breeze blows over me and I wish that I would've wore a jacket. There's not anyone on the sidewalk leading to the house but I can already see that there's a lot of people on the lawn.

I casually make my way toward the house scanning the crowd of people. From what I can see most of these people look like they're around 20 and up, I'm pretty sure I've seen some of them in the inquisitor before.

A couple of people watch me and I notice that I'm one of the only white people here -not to be rascist.- I don't see Blake anywhere and I start to become nervous.

I make my way into the house where I smell something that resembles skunk and I turn my nose up.

What the hell?

There's more people on the inside than there were on the lawn and I regret agreeing to come here. The music is blasting and I think it's some Niki Minaj song but I'm not sure.

I almost have a heart attack when someone grabs onto my arm. I slowly turn around hoping its Blake but that's not who I come face to chest with.

"Hey," Zach says with a grin on his face and I let out a breath of relief.

"You almost gave me a heart attack," I tell him punching his arm but he just grins.

"Looking for Blake?" He asks.

"Um yes," I tell him.

He points a finger towards the opposite way of where I came in from. "He's out back." He tells me and I give him a grateful smile before going that way.

I make my way through all of the people, receiving a couple of lares in the process. I finally make it to a screen door that leads to the back and I go outside.

Out here it's much more peaceful but the skunk smell is stronger. There's couples out here and a couple of people in the pool. I walk around looking for Blake and frown when I see him with making out with some girl against the house.

Wow.

I take a deep breath and try to push away the jealousy that's already forming inside of me.

"Hey you!" Someone calls out and on instant I turn around to see a group of about 5 guys huddled by a tree. There's smoke coming from where they are but when one beckons me over I walk towards them.

Hell I have nothing else to do.

All of the guys are tall and I look like a midget compared to them.

"What's your name?" One of them asks with a deep voice. I look up to see that it's the tallest guy who looks around twenty with his goatee.

I feel a little nervous but just like the jealousy I push it aside.

"Allison."

"You with Blake?" Another one asks and I look down at his hand to see he's holding a joint.

Well that explains the smoke and skunk smell.

"Yea." I say.

"Looks like he abandoned you," the guy says gesturing to where Blake is. I just shrug at the guy, "Why don't you hang with us ?"

I'm skeptical for a bit and I'm conflicted on what to do but when I see Blake I already know what my answer is going to be.

I sway my hips to the music as the guy behind me holds my hips and moves his along with mine.

I feel like a bird.

Free.

All of my stress from these last weeks are gone and I don't have any worries. "Why don't we go upstairs." The guy whispers in my ear.

Hmm, why not.

The guy grabs my hand and starts to lead me toward the stairs.

I'm shoved back as my hand is ripped away from the guy and I let out a grunt.

"What do you think your doing?" Someone yells but I don't pay them any attention.

The next thing I know someone is beating on the guy I was about to go upstairs with.

That's not nice.

I stagger over to where the guys are brawling on the ground and start to ell at them, "Hey stop it!"

No one pays any attention to me but people start to pull the guys away from each other though.

The guy who was obviously inning breaks loose of the people who were holding him and starts to make his way towards me.

Uh oh.

He looks pretty violent.

Before I can even think about it I start to run away from the guy and out the house.

"Allison!" I hear someone yell but I ignore them as I bump into people while I run.

Once I'm out of the house it's easier to avoid people and run. But I stop to decide where I'm going which is a big no no because someone grabs my shoulder and I start to scream.

A hand is placed over my mouth, "Allison stop screaming." Blake hisses spinning me around to look at him.

He looks pissed and he's gripping my shoulder pretty tightly.

"We're leaving," he says and with that he literally drags me to the car.

"I would've thought that you wouldn't touch weed again," Blake says as we pull up to my house, "after the brownies."

I don't reply to him I just cross my arms over my chest and pout.

He ruined my fun.

Blake lets out a sigh before dragging me in the house and to my room, "I have no idea why I brought you with me," he mutters, "it's pretty obvious you and parties don't mix well."

"It's pretty obvious you're an ass." I say since I'm still pissed about the girl earlier; I know we're not dating but still.

"What was that?" Blake asks as I sit on my bed and he glares at me.

"I said its pretty obvious you're an ass." I tell him, "You bring me to a oath, leave me, and then I find you making out with some girl."

I'm pretty sure the only reason I said that out loud is because of the weed.

"Why is it any of your business who I hook up with?" He says leaning against the door before he starts to smirk a little, "I told you if you want me to stop all you have to do is admit you like me." He says with an arrogant smile, "Is there anything you want to admit SweetCheeks?"

"Fine," I say standing up and marching over to him, "I Allison Darling, somehow like you," I poke him in the chest, "Blake Drayton some kind of way even though you're a complete asswhole with a huge ego problem." I say and I'm barely done with the sentence before his lips are on mine.

I'm not sure if its because of the weed of what but this feels like the best kiss ever. Our lips move in sync and its slow and gentle. Blake slowly moves us to the bed and lays me down on my back while he's above me.

I let out a grunt when he pulls away from me and looks me over. Something passes through his eyes and he seems conflicted, "Will you be my girlfriend Allison?"

It feels like all of the air leaves my lungs at his question.

Did Blake really just ask me out?

Before I can stop myself I answer him, "Yes."

Chapter 30

I let out a groan when I wake up and burry my face into my pillow.

My head hurts and I'm so hungry I could eat this house right now. What in the hell did I do last night?

I continue to just lay in my bed for a little bit until I'm able to re,e,her the events of last night.

Went to a party with Blake.

He abandoned me.

I got high with a group of guys I didn't know.

Danced with some dude.

Blake started a fight.

Humph, dumbass.

We got home and..

Aw hell, are Blake and I really dating?

I turn my head to the side and see that Blake's sleeping peacefully. I can tell he's shirtless and when I look down I realize I am too.

Hmm, how did I not notice that?

I let out a grunt and ease my way out of the bed trying not to wake Blake.

I look down at myself and realize a shirt isn't the only thing I'm missing.

Why am I so un obserbitive this morning?

I slip on some clothes and my house shoes before making my way downstairs. The only thought that's on my mind is Blake and I dating. I'm not sure of how under the influence he was last night so he may not have meant it. If he was just joking I can blame my saying "yes" on the weed.

Yea, that's what I'm going to do.

I rummage through the fridge and let out a groan when I realize there's not anything to eat.

Dammit I'm starving.

I'll just go buy something.

I head back up stairs and I'm relieved to find that Blake is still sleep. I throw on some half presentable clothes, brush my teeth, and throw my hair in a ponytail before heading outside to my car. I end up going to McDonald's since its the closest. When I start to look the menu over I know that I'm going to get a lot of stuff to eat.

"Well isn't that a lot of food,I'm guessing you got enough for me." Blake says when I return home and walk into the kitchen. He's sitting at the table with his phone in front of him, shirtless. He smirks at me as he looks at the McDonald's bags I'm holding.

"No," I tell him putting the bags on the counter.

Is he going to mention last nigh-

"Why not, aren't girlfriends suppose to go get food for their boyfriend." Blake says breaking me from my thoughts.

I guess he is going to mention it then.

Instead of answering him I simply scowl at him before taking a bite out of my hash brown.

"Oh so that's how you're going to play this," he says smirking at me as he stands up from his seat, "it's out in the open now Allison, you have feelings for me and there's no denying it." He says as he begins to walk closer to me.

I back up against the counter and his grin widens. As he walks closer I begin to remember he's shirtless and has a really nice body.

"I don't know what you're talking about." I tell him playing clueless as I finish chewing and let my hand that's holding the rest of the hash brown fall loosely at my side.

Blake doesn't stop walking until our bodies are firmly pressed against each other, "So your going to play dumb," he says as he begins to twirl a piece of my hair around his finger absently.

"Blake we were both intoxicated last night." I tell him.

A light smile makes its way into his face and he shakes his head, "No, I was completely sober, and you're sober now so tell me did you mean what you said last night?" He continues to twirl my hair as if its normal, "If not we'll act like nothing ever happened." His green eyes begin to pierce my blue ones.

I guess I have to be honest or we'll never get anywhere, "Yes," I finally say and Blake smiles as he tugs my lips towards his by the strand of hair he'd been twirling. The kiss is gentle, slow, and makes me want to melt on the spot. Blake pulls away first and smirks at me, he snatches my hash brown out of my hand before giving me a quick peck on the lips and retreating out of the kitchen.

He did not just still my hash brown.

That ass whole.

"Blake get back here!" I yell running after him.

"So you're finally dating?" Jasmine asks with a smirk when Blake and I arrive to school Wednesday. Her and Will had been standing by the vending machine arguing over who got to go first but now their attention was fully directed at us.

"Can't I at least get a hi or hello?" I ask sarcastically rolling my eyes at her.

"Hey, hi, are you two really finally dating?" She asks repeating her question as her gaze flickers between the two of us.

Blake just smirks and I know he's waiting for me to tell her yes. We'd road to school together this morning since he's still at my house but since I called my dad yesterday he pulled some strings and got two plane tickets for our mom's to get back today meaning out housemate time is going to come to an end soon.

"So?" Jasmine asks as she begins to become impatient.

I scratch the back of my head before letting out a sigh, "Yes." The words barely out of my mouth before Jasmine's jumping for joy and squealing causing a lot of people to look at us.

Blake chuckles at her reaction and Will uses this moment to get something from the vending machine. Just as his drink his the bottom where you get it from Jasmine stops squealing and snatches it up, "Thanks honey bunchkins." She says causing Will to let out a grunt.

Huh, I wonder if they're official now?

Jasmine loops her arm through mine, "Bye boys, see you in first hour." She says giving them a wave before dragging me away from them.

"Did you miss school yesterday because y'all were having hot steamy sex?" Is her first question and I almost choke on air.

"No," I tell her, "I was dealing with side affects front eh party the night before." I tell her as a thought occurs to me, "How did you know about us anyway?" I ask her since I hadn't had time to tell her.

She gives me a smile, "Blake told Will and he told me." She explains.

I nod my head before turning to her, "Speaking of which, are you two dating now?" I ask since she'd called him 'honey bunchkins' earlier.

She lets out an unamused snort, "No, sorry we can't all have a nice little fairy tale life." She says, "We're just sort of friends, I guess." She says in an unsure tone.

"You mea-"

"Yes, we're done with all the benefits and stuff," she says, "the only thing hot between us is our arguments."

"What happened?" I ask since obviously something must have got inbetweeen them.

She shrugs, "I'm a whore, he's a man whore, and jealousy kept getting in the way." She explains with a sigh.

"Sorry," I say but she just shrugs.

"Obviously there was never going to be anything more than sex between us."

I let out a sigh, "Alright, lets go to first hour."

Chapter 31

"Well I can't say that I'm not surprised the house isn't a mess," my mother says when she enters our house and takes a look around.

I roll my eyes and notice that she got tanner while gone.

Guess they went down south.

"I'm going out tonight so Blake will be coming over." She tells me as I follow her into the kitchen.

Is she serious?

I thought they'd gambled all their money.

"With what money mom?" I ask her.

She shrugs her shoulders, "Your dad sent me some money and I want to spend it as quick as I can." She tells me and I shake my head.

Does she really despise dad that much?

I mean he's not my favorite person, and he cheated on her but he's giving her money, she should be happy about that.

"Okay, whatever." I tell her as I sit down on the stool.

She starts to go through cabinets looking for stuff and when she tenses I know something's wrong.

Hmm. What have I put in the cabinet lately?

I check which cabinet she's in and realize its the medicine one.

Oh hell.

"Allison, what's this?" She asks turning to me with my birth control in her hand. I know she knows what it is she just wants an explanation from me.

I scratch the back of my neck as I hear our front door open.

I silently pray to the big an upstairs that the person will be able to distract my mom.

When Blake and his mom walk in I know that my prayers haven't been answered.

"Are those birth control pills?" Blake's mom asks when she looks at my mom's hand.

Kill me now.

"Yes," my mom says, "now Allison, why are these in my cabinet?"

"Uh.." I glance at Blake who has a blank look on his face but I can tell he's nervous by the way he keeps clenching and unclenching his hands.

"Don't uh me," she says crossing her arms over her chest.

"Well, I've been active," I tell her awkwardly, "and I'm just taking precautions." I finally manage to say.

"And who have you been active with?" She asks.

My eyes are traitors and flicker to Blake before I look at the ground.

"Blake Drayton." I here his mom yell and I look up to see her glaring at him, "I always knew you were a man whore, but my best friend's daughter, really?"

"Mom." Blake says letting out a groan as he slips into a seat beside me.

"Do we need to have the talk?" My mom asks and I almost die on the spot.

"No mom," I say putting my head in my hands, "I know about sex and the consequences." I tell her but I don't mention that we almost had a scare about me being pregnant.

"So, are you two dating then?" Blake's mom asks.

Blake runs a hand through his hair, "Yea." He says with a nod of his head and our mom's both smile.

"So when did you start dating?" My mom asks as she leans forward looking at us.

This is going to be a long day.

After our mom's finally stopped pestering us Blake told me there was somewhere he needed to take me so we headed out.

When we finally reach our destination I realize its the place we'd visited after we left "The Grill."

"Why are we here?" I ask staring at the warehouse.

"Allison, there's something I need to tell you," he says turning to me with a serious expression that he rarely has.

"What?" I ask bringing my eyebrows together in confusion.

What could be so serious that he needs to tell me?

"I'm..." He trails off unable to finish his sentence.

I watch him as I wait for the end of his sentence.

He finally takes a deep breath and spits out what he was going to say, "I'm in a gang." He finally says.

"You've got to be kidding me," I say, "You know that idea had once gone through my head when everyone was like he's a bad boy." I tell him with a shake of my head, "but then I was like nah he's too wimpy." I explain disappointed that I hadn't put together that he's in a gang.

Blake just stares at me in shock, "You took this pretty well considering I thought you were going to break up with me and run for the hills."

"Why would I do that?"

He simply shakes his head at me and gets out of the car, "Come on." He calls out to me and I follow him into the warehouse.

We go through a couple of hallways and doors before we end up in a room where I see Zach, and Will. Should've known they were int his gang too.

Will almost has a heart attack when he sees me since he was in the middle of making out with some blond. Guess he thinks I'm going to tell Jaz, even though they technically don't have anything.

"Hey Allison." Zach says with a smirk.

"Hey," I tell him before I look at some of the people in the room and realize I saw them at the party the other night.

"Blake, Julian wants to see you." A guy says sticking his head in the room. Blake nods at him and the guy leaves.

Blake frowns as he looks at me, "We'll keep an eye on her." Will whispers when he walks up to us and grabs my arm.

With one last glance at me Blake leaves the room.

"So Allison, has Jasmine been hanging with a lot of guys?" Will asks casually and I smirk.

Chapter 32

I t's been four weeks since Blake and I started dating. Not much has really changed, we still argue and bicker but we kiss, a lot: which usually leads to something more. Our moms's are still partying and gambling: at least they're in our city. Will and Jasmine have started to avoid each other at all cost, but if you ask them, they'd deny it.

The worst that's happened these last few weeks though is that Blake's becoming distant. I don't mean to sound like a clingy girlfriend or something, because I'm definitely not one, but it's been weird. One minute we're in the middle of making out and he gets a text or call so he leaves. He's been like this every since we went to the warehouse. I'm really starting to wonder if he keeps running off to his sideline flings or something.

"What are you thinking so hard about?" Jasmine asks me as she throws me a basketball.

We're currently at basketball practice, and we're obviously suppose to be working on drills but my mind's in other places.

"Nothing." I tell her as I shoot the ball and miss; that's a first. Jasmine shoots me a strange look but she doesn't make any comments.

"Do you think Blake's cheating on me?" I ask her out of the blue as we're leaving practice, and heading to the student parking lot.

Jasmine stops walking and turns to look at me with a frown, "Why would you think that?"

I give her a shrug, "He's always running off, and we still haven't even had an official date." I explain as her eyes focus on something behind me.

I try to search her face as she's looking behind me to see if she gives anything away, since her and Blake have been hanging out a lot lately. Hell, she's been spending more time with him than me and Will do. So if anyone knows something it'll be her, even though I think she would've told me.

She lets out a sigh, "Alli, I'm pretty sure he isn't cheating." Her eyes flicker back to me.

"Who isn't cheating?" A husky voice asks causing me to turn and see Blake. He's dressed in a pair of ripped jeans and a tight black tee that shows off his abs and muscles.

"Chandler from friends." Jasmine says, the lie rolling off her tongue easily.

"Oh," Blake says but I know he doesn't believe her.

"Okay well I'll text you guys later." Jasmine says as her and Blake lock eyes for a second before she quickly jogs off to her car.

Weird.

Blake frowns for a second as he watches her leave before turning to me with a smirk.

"We're going out tonight," he says as he guides me to his car.

"Where?" I ask with a frown as I get into the passenger seat.

"It's a surprise date, so I'm not telling you." He says as he gets into the car and cranks it.

"Are you serious?" I ask wondering if he overheard Jasmine and I's conversation.

"Yea, it's about time." He says before looking at the clock on his dashboard, "We can actually go now if you want." He tells me.

"Uh, I'm sweaty, and I have on practice clothes." I tell him with a frown.

"Your point?" He asks.

I let out a sigh knowing that he's going to insist on us going, "Okay." I tell him and he gives me a smug smile.

I glance around me at the fancy scenery wondering why in the hell Blake brought me here in these clothes. Hell, I thought we were going to go to McDonalds or something.

"Right this way," the hostess says leasing us to our booth as she gives Blake a flirtatious smile. I roll my eyes at her but I don't say anything since Blake isn't even looking at her.

"Your waiter will be with you in a little bit." She tells us as we sit at a booth made for two people int the back of the restaurant.

"So do you like this place?" Blake asks me as he picks up his menu.

"It's amazing," I tell him and he simply smiles as our waiter appears at our table.

He takes our drinks and our orders.

"So w-" Blake's sentence is cut off as his phone rings. He picks up the phone and frowns before answering, "Yea?" He pauses as he listens to the person on the other line, "I can't.." He glances at me, "No.. Okay, fine." He slams his phone shut and I let out a sigh knowing what's coming next."

"I'm sorr-"

I cut him off before he can even apologize, "Okay, whatever." I say knowing he's bailing on me.

Again.

"I'm really sorry," he digs in his pocket to pull out a wad of cash, "Look, I'll get Will to come pick you up." He says making me even more pissed.

First he brings me on this awesome date and then bails on me.

Second he doesn't even explain why he's leaving.

And lastly he isn't even taking me home, he's getting someone else to do it.

A pleading and hurt look makes its way onto his face."Allison, I really am s-"

I cut him off with a wave of my hand before turning my head.

I hear him let out a sigh before he walks over and gives me a kiss on the cheek.

Then he leaves.

I feel like a loner as I sit by myself at the restaurant with two plates of food sitting in front of me. A lot of people look at me with pity and I have the urge to flip them off but I don't.

"Is this seat taken?" Someone asks and I recognize the voice instantly.

I look up from my plate at Will who's giving me an apologetic smile.

"No, whatever, just sit." I tell him as I let out a sigh.

He sits across from me, "Let us always meet each other with a smile, for the smile is the beginning of love."

I give Will a strange look as he gives me a genuine smile, "What the hell?"

"I don't know," he says with a shrug, "I'm trying to get you to smile." He says and in spite of myself I smile.

"Where did you even get that stupid quote from anyway?" I ask him as I roll my eyes.

He smirks, "That mother woman."

"Moth Teresa?" I ask and he nods as he stuffs the pasta that Blake had ordered into his mouth.

"You should eat," he says pointing his fork at my food.

With a sigh I start to slowly eat my shrimp.

Once we're done eating Will drives me home and he follows me inside the house since he's made it his goal to "make me feel better" or whatever.

"What movies do you have?" He asks as we make our way upstairs to my room.

I shrug my shoulders, "They're all inside my closet on the top shelf." I tell him and he goes to my closet to pick a movie out.

He comes back out with a BRATZ movie making my eyes widen.

He looks at my face with a frown, "What? I love this movie, my sister use to make me watch it all the time." He says putting the movie into the DVD player. "You better not tell anyone either." He says as he lays in the bed next to me, but there's a good amount of space between us.

"Of course," I tell him with a small smile on my face.

All through the movie I can't help but laugh, Will starts to get excited whenever stuff happens in the movie ad he sometimes just tickles me in a friendly way to make me smile. Halfway through the movie my phone rings and I glance down to see Blake's name on the caller ID.

"He's probably calling to apologize." Will says as he pauses the movie, "put him on speaker so I can hear how whipped he is." He tells me and I shake my head as I answer the phone and put it on speaker.

"Hell-" my greeting is cut short when I hear Blake on the other.

"We can't let Allison find out," he says and my heart starts to beat frantically in my chest as I hear a smacking sound that resembles a kiss.

"Of course not," a feminine voice says and I swear my heart breaks.

I glance at Will who's frowning and sending me an apologetic look.

"I'll break up with her next week," Blake says and I feel a tear roll down my face.

"Okay, I think she's suspicious anyway." The girl says and when I realize who it is my whole world shatters.

The girl is Jasmine.

Chapter 33

I wake up to a leg thrown over mines and an arm around my bare torso. My head's pounding like I've been hit in the head with a sludge hammer repeatedly.

The person lets out a groan before sitting up, "What happened?" Will asks as the covers fall off revealing his naked chest. He runs a hand through his hand as I try to remember what exactly happened last night.

12 HOURS EARLIER

After I hear Jasmine's voice I'm just in shock as I start to cry. Looking at Will's face I know he's feeling the same way I am. Instead of crying though he picks up the phone and silently hangs it up.

The next thing I know Will has his arm wrapped around me in a warm embrace. He just holds me while I cry without saying anything. I'm not crying because of Blake, I've always known that he's an ass. I'm crying because my best friend for years betrayed me. Out of all the people I never would have thought that Jasmine would do this to me. I should have picked up on the signs: the hanging out a lot, the secretive looks, texting a lot. I guess I thought that I could trust them.

Guess I was wrong.

"Don't cry over someone who wouldn't cry over you." Will finally says breaking me out of my thoughts as he gently wipes a tear away.

I let out a sob as I help him wipe my tears, "I'm not crying over him." I say as I realize when I went to see my doctor a couple of weeks ago she told me I didn't need anymore stress in my life.

"Well don't cry over her either," he says as he turns me to face him, "A true friend would never make you cry." He tells me and even though I know he means his words there's sadness in his eyes.

I know he's right but I just can't stop crying.

"I know what'll make you feel better." He says as he stands up and grabs my hands.

"What?" I ask as I let him help me up.

"Partying, and alcohol."

The bass of the speakers in the club causes vibrations under my feet as Will leads me to the bar. I was surprised when he led me to Winters's Cade (the place where Blake and I had once came.) Instead of going to the part that is an arcade though he took me to the club part that Blake told me about.

"What can I get you two?" The bartender asks with a friendly smile on his face.

"Two vodka shots," Will tells the man and he nods before pouring us two shots.

I throw the shot back feeling a burning sensation deep in my throat. Will orders another round and after a while the burning doesn't even faze me.

"Lets dance," I tell Will slurring my words.

"Okay!" He basically shouts and jumps off of the bar still stumbling a little. He leads me off to the dance floor and we start dancing to some fast beat song. I end up grinding on Will and he encourages me as he places his hands on my hips and starts to grind his pelvis against me.

A slower song comes on and I turn around wrapping my arms around his neck and he places his hands around my waist pulling me to him.

"We should get revenge." Will says when he learns down to my ear level.

"We should!" I tell him wondering if he can hear me over the music.

We don't discuss the revenge thing any further as we continue to dance against each other.

We stumble into my house a couple of hours later since the bouncer kicked us out.

I trip over some imaginary misplaced thing and Will grabs my shoulders catching me. He spins me around and we come face to face. "Are you okay?" He asks as his eyes wonder to my lips.

"Yea..." I mutter before crashing my lips to his.

Will doesn't waste any time before he kisses me back. He rubs his hands up and down my back. He slides his hands to my butt before picking me up and carrying me up the stairs not ever breaking the kiss.

He gently lays me on the bed and we continue to kiss. His tongue slips into my mouth as I give him entrance while my hands run through my hair.

"Hey," I mutter as Will starts to suck on my neck.

"Mm hmm," is the only reply I get.

"Maybe we should use this as our revenge." I say as I roll us over so I'm straddling him and he's looking up at me.

"How so?" He asks as he continues to rub my back.

I shrug as I tug his shirt over his head, "A recording, or call them." I say as I began to run my hands over his abs causing him to shiver.

He gently pulls my face down to him by my hair as he begins to work on my neck again, "Which one would we call?" He asks before his tongue flicks out tickling the sensitive skin on my neck and my whole body heats up.

"Both," I say as I push him back and start to kiss his neck causing him to let out a moan. "I'll call one you call the other." I tell him in-between the kisses.

"Or I can call them both on our phones while you continue to do that." He says.

"Mmhm," I tell him as he grabs his phone out of his pocket.

"Where's your phone?" He asks a little breathless.

"Back pocket," I tell him as I start to kiss down his chest.

He lets out a groan before reaching into the back pockets of my shorts. His hand lingers for a bit before he slowly slides his hand out and I know he's doing it on purpose.

I hear beeps as he begins to call them. All of a sudden he quickly turns us over stripping my shirt off.

Guess he's done with the phone.

He runs his hands slowly over my breast causing me to moan out loudly.

Next he slides my shorts off and smirks at me as he looks at my woman hood.

We're definitely about to give Jasmine and Blake the best recording of their lives.

"Whoa," Will says and I guess he just remembered last night like I did.

"Yea," I say running a hand through my hair, "You don't suppose we could go for a round two, do you?" I ask and he smiles at me.

"I definitely wouldn't object but I'm sure Blake will be over in a bit." He tells me glancing at my alarm clock, "I'm really surprised he isn't her-" Will's sentence cuts off as the door bangs open revealing a red faced and angry Blake, Jasmine comes in behind him and I can't even look at her.

"What in the hell do you think you're doing?" Blake yells at us but his anger's more directed at Will.

"Look," Will says running a hand through his hair, "I know it's a fight you want so let me throw my boxers on and then we can fight it out." He says and for once he isn't the bubbly happy person he usually is. He looks like he's ready to kick Blake's ass.

I really hope he does.

"Don't know why you need to cover up," Blake growls out, "Everyone else has seen you exposed." He says before sending me a glare.

Will just sends him a cold smile, "Get out." He says and for a second I think Blake isn't going to back out but him and Jasmine leave the room.

Will stands up fully naked before locating his boxers.

I watch him for a second before getting out of the bed myself and getting dressed in my underwear and a big t-shirt. I can't avoid the devils for too long.

Will and I walk downstairs together and Blake barely lets us walk into the kitchen before he attacks Will. Apparently Will was expecting this because he doesn't seem too fazed about the punch to the cheek Blake landed on him. He recovers before he punches Blake back hard and I hear something crack.

Ha that's what that ass gets.

They both end up rolling around and hitting each her on the floor. It's really hard to tell who's winning and I don't think the fight is ever going to be broken up before Jasmine lets out a sigh and starts to make her way over to them.

She looks at me with stress in her eyes, "Are you going to help?"

"You can't be seriously talking to me." I hiss crossing my arms over my chest.

She lets out a sigh running a hand through her hair, "Allison please don't, you don't understand." She sounds frustrated and worried at the same time.

Just because I don't want my mom to throw a fit when she gets home I help her pull them apart. Let me tell you these two are strong as hell but they'd never hit a girl, even if Blake is a cheating ass hole.

I can barely look at Blake and Jasmine who stand on one side of the room while Will and I stand on the other. Will and Blake are both bloody and bruised.

"Get out of my house!" I yell at them pointing towards the door.

"You can't possibly be mad at us for nothing when you two fucking slept together!" Blake yells and my anger boils.

"Maybe you should check your call history and see who you speed dialed, now get out!" I yell again before grabbing Will's wrist and dragging him upstairs to my bathroom.

"Sit." I instruct him pointing to the counter as I get the first aid kit out.

"Allis-"

"No." I say cutting him off as I start to cry again, "I don't want your sympathy."

He just lets out a sigh as he grabs my wrist when I start to clean his face.

He pulls me into a hug and just lets me cry.

Epilogue

It's been two weeks since the "accident" (yes that's what I'm calling it.) I haven't talked to Jasmine or Blake. I try to even avoid Jasmine at games and practices. Unfortunately I still have to sit by Blake in most of my classes. Will and I haven't hooked up again since a couple of days after the accident. We're better as friends and we were both just rebounding, plus I'm not Jasmine so I don't date my best f-, ex best friend's ex boyfriend. My mom and Blake's mom are oblivious to the fact that we don't associate anymore since they're always questioning me about our relationship.

I let out a sigh as I push my thoughts away as I walk into the deserted coffee house. There's only a couple of people and they're all adults. I walk up to the counter where a girl is smiling at me.

"What can I get you today?" She asks.

I glance at the door when I hear the bell chime and I look away when I see Blake coming in. I haven't mentioned but over the last weeks he's sort of gone caveman. He hasn't shaved so he has stubble on his face that makes him look older and he always looks so mopey like now he's looking at the ground.

I guess he feels my eyes on him because he looks up. There seems to be an internal debate going on with him because he keeps looking between me and the door. He finally continues to walk towards the register.

"Ma'am." The girl says and I look back at her to see she's patiently waiting for me to order.

"Oh," I say running a hand through my hair, "a large caramel frappe extra cool whip and syrup." I tell her as I go in my wallet.

"Make that two," a husky voice says and I get a whiff of cologne that smells quite good.

The girl looks behind me but without the dazed look that she gets I know it's Blake,"Okay, that will be seven ninety five." She says no longer looking at me as her smile widens.

I glance behind me to see Blake pulling out a ten and giving it to her.

"Your number is 98." She says passing Blake a receipt before starting on the drinks.

Blake and I wait in silence for our drinks neither one of us saying anything. I don't even say anything about him adding his stuff onto my ticket and paying.

"Here you go." The girl says passing us our drinks, "have a nice day."

Blake gives her a nod but I almost miss it since I started to leave as soon as I grab my coffee.

Just as I'm about to open my car door I'm stopped by a warm hand on my wrist.

"Allison," he says so softly I almost just melt and forgive him.

I close my eyes collecting myself before turning around and glaring at him.

"Allison, please don't, you don't understand."

His words remind me of what Jasmine said the day after the accident when Blake and Will were fighting.

Anger starts to boil in me, "Well please explain to me Blake, how could you cheat on me with my best friend?" I ask as I feel tears pool in my eyes.

He looks down at me with the saddest look I've ever seen him wear, "Allison I didn't mean to hurt you." He says as he pulls me into a hug.

For some reason I just let him hold me for a little bit. Maybe it's because deep down I still have feelings for him (well maybe not that deep) or maybe I need it for closure. I'm sure it's the former though.

I finally pull back and look him dead in the eyes as a single tear escapes, "Well you did hurt me." I tell him before getting in my car and driving away.

"Allison honey," my mom say as she enters my room a few hours later, I've been in here moping and crying ever since I left the coffee house.

"What?" I ask turning my head to look at her.

She has a happy glint in her eyes even though I know she trying to hide it, "I need for you to come downstairs." She tells me before turning and leaving.

I let out a groan why couldn't she tell me what she needed to say up here. I trudge down the stairs and go into the kitchen where I find her, Beatrice, and surprisingly Blake.

Mom and Beatrice look cheerful for some odd reason.

I sit on one of the bar stools avoiding Blake's piercing gaze.

Blake finally looks away from me, "Why are we here?" He asks and I'm guessing they dragged him here too.

"We won the lottery!" My mom and Beatrice both yell at the same time causing me to whip my head up.

"You mean you lost the lottery right?" I ask skeptically looking at them.

"No silly," my mom says, "we finally won."

Okay, this is weird.

"So why did you call this group meeting, couldn't you have told up separately?" Blake questions.

"Because, we're going on a cruise for six months." Beatrice says and I know this isn't going to end well.

"Are we going too?" Blake asks.

"Of course not," my mom says, "You two are moving into a new house and staying together.